Ben Woolfenden's career has included stints
as a local government officer, a songwriter,
and an unloader of frozen doughnuts in a cold
storage warehouse. Eight years ago he became
a bookseller, and until recently was deputy
manager of a bookshop in Covent Garden.
The Ruins of Time is his first novel. Ben
Woolfenden is now writing full time and
working on a second novel. *The Ruins of Time*
has been selected for the W.H. Smith First
Novels Promotion.

The Ruins of Time

Ben Woolfenden

BLACK SWAN

THE RUINS OF TIME
A BLACK SWAN BOOK 0 552 99500 2

First publication in Great Britain

PRINTING HISTORY
Black Swan edition published 1993

Set in 11pt Linotype Melior by
County Typesetters, Margate, Kent.

Black Swan Books are published by Transworld Publishers Ltd,
61–63 Uxbridge Road, Ealing, London W5 5SA, in Australia
by Transworld Publishers (Australia) Pty Ltd, 15–23 Helles Avenue,
Moorebank, NSW 2170, and in New Zealand by Transworld
Publishers (NZ) Ltd, 3 William Pickering Drive, Albany, Auckland.

Printed and bound in Great Britain by
Cox & Wyman Ltd, Reading, Berks.

For Geoffrey Downes

The ruins of Time build mansions in Eternity

William Blake

Part One

Chapter One

Past midnight in the darkened house, its silence resounding with the ticking of clocks, and my father still
hard at work. Through the open door of the study I see
him seated in an ancient leather armchair, bent forward, pen poised, to peer into a yellow cone of light,
suspended from the Anglepoise on the desk before
him. Within its glare lie the paraphernalia of his hobby
turned obsession – a magnifying glass, dusty books,
dog-eared papers and files piled high. In the shadowy
alcoves beyond him, overburdened shelves extend
from floor to ceiling; on the wall a cork notice board, to
which are pinned sepia-tinted photographs, addresses,
telephone numbers, reminders to himself. Blue and
motionless tails of pipe smoke hang in the still air.

And this consuming passion, this late-night dedication is for extinct facts, disinterred from official
registers of births, deaths and marriages, grave-robbed
from censuses and newspaper archives, from the
diaries of those long since under the earth. Dead facts,
except in the eyes of my father, who dreams of filling
forgotten places with a host of unremembered people –
to bring them all back to life.

I bid him good night from the unlit hallway, fatally
breaking his concentration, for he beckons me within,
suddenly eager to share his discoveries. And I concur,
resigning myself to the postponement of sleep.

His tiredness miraculously vanishes: those eyes, dulled by age and a surfeit of small print, are suddenly illuminated by his fervour for the subject, conveying the potency of his imagination. He sits back, lights his pipe, asks me to consider a possible version of events. I listen and find myself captivated by the story he constructs from lifeless facts.

Chapter Two

Picture an area of countryside in Lancashire, as it might appear today. There is a metalled road running between large fields. Beyond these, dark moorlands sweep to the horizon. A group of farm buildings stands a little way from the road; in the farmyard there are tractors, modern machines. Now I want you to annihilate certain things from your image. First, take away the road and that old lorry which is labouring up it; in its place put a rutted cart track. Then erase those telegraph poles, with their swooping wires which follow the road's progress. Lift those electricity pylons from the skyline, dissolve the farm buildings made of concrete, corrugated iron and brick, and plant a small, stone-built farmstead in their place. Where you saw tractors, see pony carts. Then create a patchwork of smaller fields, partitioned by neat hedgerows, and beyond those a huddle of thatched and decrepit cottages close to an inn and a small church. Perhaps the sun is shining in your picture. Blot it out with a mist, for it is very early on a September morning. The year is 1830.

On tiptoe you can just see into that field close by, where a small ragged boy is running wildly over the ploughed earth, waving his arms and whooping at the top of his voice. At his approach, waves of dark birds rise in whiplashes into the air and wheel across the sodden skies.

Study the boy's face, his expression of enthusiasm (for he enjoys this scaring labour). The crucial importance of the few pennies he is paid each day by the landowner is not yet apparent to him. Although he shivers and his clothes and boots are badly worn and patched, he is momentarily happy as the unchallenged ruler of this tiny kingdom.

When he is hungry in the middle of the day he eats a hunk of bread and a much smaller one of cheese, and feeling the need for more food, is bitterly unhappy that it is denied him. But once he resumes his work for the afternoon he forgets the emptiness which seizes his stomach, for in his life he has rarely experienced the pleasure of eating his fill.

As dusk falls, his day's crow-scaring done, he makes his way to the farmer's warm and well-stocked kitchen to collect his wage. Through the doorway he glimpses a stone-flagged floor, washed by firelight, trays of warm bread upon a large table of polished oak, two rabbit carcasses hanging from hooks in the ceiling beams.

On receiving his payment, the boy, whose name is William Daniels, offers repeated thanks, remembering his mother's warning that gratitude is imperative if he is to be granted work on the following day. And his earnings, paltry though they may be, are essential to supplement his father's occasional wages. The family has come to rely increasingly on the pitiful amount of poor relief begrudgingly dispensed by the wealthier members of the parish. In short, they cannot sink much further into destitution without, quite literally, starving to death.

As darkness deepens and a storm amasses itself in the

western sky, William follows a cart track for a short distance until he reaches the small village called Hades. At the door of the tavern he pauses and peers cautiously into the gloomy interior, where he sees his father, Bartholomew Daniels, amongst a group of men seated at a corner table. William has long realized that his father's labour is hired less and less frequently, and that as a consequence he is to be found in this tavern more and more, where to win at cards ensures the price of a drink.

The boy stands timidly in the doorway, until he is noticed by his father. From experience, William anticipates one of two possible outcomes: if his father is losing at cards and is only half-drunk as a result, he will be sworn at and waved away; if, on the other hand, his father's luck is in, and his mood is merry, he will be beckoned within, to sit quietly with the group of men for a short while.

Let us assume that on this September evening William is invited into the candlelit tavern, where it is warm and noisy after the day-long still and chillness of the fields. A fire is burning in the hearth, and on this occasion a side of mutton is being roasted on a spit. The spit is turned by a contraption of pulleys and wheels, in which a wretched dog is imprisoned to provide the driving force. When the animal fails to turn the spit, it is roused by the wrath of an ancient, yet dauntingly muscular landlord. The madness he has acquired through years of drinking his own poisonous liquor is vented in oaths, curses and kicks aimed at the dog. Terror awakens it from its stupor, and it turns the wheel again.

Gradually the meat begins to cook; its aroma fills the tavern tantalizingly. And then, beset by an even greater torture, the dog starts to whine and whimper at its fate – always to smell the tender meat, which will never pass its lips. So the sight of the dog fills William with sadness; he also knows that it is pointless for him to share in the longing.

Now feeling the weight of tiredness from his long day's labours, William is dozing at his father's side and is listening, half in a dream, to the conversations around him. The men speak with dread of the coming winter; of the rising prices of beer and gin; of their dislike of the local squires and landowners; and of some dimly-remembered golden age, which existed before the richer farmers bought out their poorer neighbours and enclosed the common land behind sturdy hedges. Then in hushed, dark tones – for the death penalty hovers over such things – there are tales brought by travellers of revolt in the south, of the uprising of agrarian workers, of rick-burning, machine-wrecking, murder and cattle-maiming, and of the mysterious power behind all this – the fearless Captain Swing, vengeful warrior of the poor and oppressed.

The men speculate on his identity, as a great man fallen low, or as a common man who would be great. As William dozes on the wooden bench he sees Captain Swing transformed in a dream into an enraged giant, striding at night through a moonlit landscape, hurling ploughs and threshing machines at the stars, whilst hayricks and farmsteads explode with bolts of fire from his fingertips. He wakes to see only the earnest faces, with their sunken eyes and cheeks, their tallow skin, their mouths murmuring to each other in awe.

At length his father rouses him to send him home,

first taking charge of the pennies which William has been clutching in his hand. He runs along a lane of frozen mud, under a frosty, star-filled night, until he reaches a tiny one-roomed cottage. Here a single candle burns, illuminating bare walls, their whitewash several decades old, a mud floor and two grimy rush-bottomed chairs, one of which is occupied by a frail, asthmatic woman, who scolds him for his lateness, and curses him when she learns that he has yielded his wage to her husband. An old deal table and a few pots and pans by the hearth – in which a small fire is dying – complete the scene.

William's mother raises herself from a stool before the fire and ladles a few spoonfuls of cold vegetable soup into a bowl. Once William has eaten this he curls up, fully-clothed, on a dank mattress in the corner, which he shares with his parents. But before the candle is extinguished, he peers into a wooden cot which stands beside the fireplace, staring intently at the red and puckered face of his two-month-old brother, who has only a few more days to live.

Let five years rush onwards for William, in a constant round of crow-scaring, of gleaning corn and potatoes, of gathering wild berries when food at home is in desperately short supply, of driving cattle and working on harvests, of dawns and dusks and seasons spent with the constant companion of hunger.

At the end of those turning years we must pause momentarily, now that William is ten years old, to witness the night of his mother's death. Back once more at the dilapidated cottage, we are able to see that she lies motionless on the filthy mattress, reduced by pneumonia to little more than a choking bundle of rags. What we cannot see is the swarm of rats which pours from Bartholomew Daniels's imagination, to swamp his wife's body and turn the floor into a soft black seething mass, amidst which he stamps his feet and tries to beat back the relentless tide with a broom. There now appears in the doorway the black and demoniac – at least in Bartholomew's mind – figure of the village parson, at whom he hurls chairs, pots, pans and abuse. William stands helplessly by the parson's side, having raced to him in horror through a starless, wind-howling night. Both are transfixed by the leaping shadows, the obscene and blasphemous cries of the madman who stands between them and the body. Yet in this scene of mayhem, nothing is more terrifying to William than the sudden deathly silence of his mother.

Then pause again on a winter's night a few weeks later, William's mother having been safely laid to rest in a pauper's grave, when his father fails to return to the cottage from the tavern. And so to the day that follows, during which William searches for him in vain.

From first light William wanders throughout the village and the surrounding countryside, asking those he meets if they have seen his father. He learns of no sightings. When he returns to the farm to present himself for work he is cursed for not appearing at dawn, and as an admonishment is sent away for the rest of the day.

Left alone, anxiously awaiting his father's return, he passes the hours in the cottage without food or fuel. He slips into a stupor induced by cold and hunger, as he sits beside the extinct fire. Now and then he runs his hands through his thick brown hair, sometimes scooping a louse into the palm of his hand, studying it as it furiously paddles its legs, like a minuscule boat full of vigorous rowers.

But at nightfall he is visited by the parson and an elderly, thin-faced woman attired in a long black dress. They bring bread and cheese for him. The woman remains silent, save for an occasional disdainful sniff at the condition of the room, whilst the parson interrogates the boy as to the possible whereabouts of his father. Then he draws the woman aside, turning his back to William and speaking in low tones. During this private confabulation she merely nods in agreement, and William is able to catch only a few phrases here and there.

'. . . probably gone for good at last . . . a child could not possibly understand . . . mortal sin of intoxication . . . a need for charity . . . consider a place in the workhouse . . .'

Then the parson, regarding William benignly down his hooked nose, announces that certain matters will be put in hand, should his father fail to return by the following Sunday.

Dawn provides a fine cold drizzle, to greet William after a sleepless night. When he passes by the tavern on the way to the farm he finds a group of men huddled together in the early morning gloom, waiting for the hiring to begin. The landlord of the tavern leans against the wall; William pushes through the crowd and tugs at his sleeve.

'What's a workhouse?' he asks.

'Workhouse!' the landlord guffaws, revealing black chipped teeth, before he seizes William by the throat.

'That's where they lock up cheeky little bastards, then beat 'em and starve 'em to death.'

All the men roar with laughter, and William flees in tears to start his day's work.

Let us be quite clear about William's fate, if he is to be despatched by the philanthropic parish overseers to a workhouse in the nearest town. In the fourth and fifth decades of the nineteenth century the poor of England were subjected to a tyrant more ruthless than any squire or landowner they had previously encountered. The enactment of the Workhouse System, born in 1834, passed through Parliament with a face beaming with enlightenment; but by the time it appeared in the towns and fields of the country, it had assumed an expression of savage despotism.

Through the newly-wrought iron gates the men, women and children were herded; then the husbands were separated from wives, the mothers from children. All paupers were deprived of adequate nourishment; all were made to work at exhausting labours, grinding bones or glass from dawn to dusk; physical violence, or imprisonment in the workhouse cage, without food or water, awaited those who voiced their protests; unmarried mothers were humiliated by being forced to wear a yellow badge of shame. Over all, silence, discipline, despair, cruelty, and, inevitably, death hovered: the cost, in human misery, of saving the ratepayers a million a year. As my father – who has dedicated most of his life to the lessons of history – points out to me, we might as well be looking at a prototype for Auschwitz, a century before its realization.

Are we to conclude that William dies in the workhouse, his life curtailed by cholera or pneumonia, breathing his last in a dungeon with barred windows? Or do we see him being put out to work for a factory master? He is, after all, able-bodied, although he is physically too developed (fortunately for him) to be chosen for that most dreadful apprenticeship of all: chimney boy to a master sweep. Whatever – a life of enslavement will certainly begin for him. He will start work at five o'clock in the morning, and will not finish until seven or eight o'clock at night, following this pattern for six days a week, for fifty weeks of the year.

Imprisoned all these days within the spinning mill's walls, tending and cleaning the cacophonous machines which never cease their giddying motions, he will be sapped of strength and willpower by undernourishment and plain cruelty. Each afternoon he will feel so exhausted, his ability to concentrate on his work will be spent; and having no family at work by his side, he will be persecuted by a sadistic overseer. What horrors we could imagine! – to find that William is to be flogged severely, or hung upside down by his feet above that deafening machinery, or locked in a small cupboard, for committing the smallest of misdemeanours. Such destinies for William would be entirely credible, and yet – and I picture my father shaking his head – we know that a different fate, in short, a kind of salvation, now awaits the boy.

So we find him sitting by the lane's side, a little way from the village, halfway through his day's labours, with nothing to eat and his thoughts filled with images of the nameless terrors which await him at the workhouse. For these reasons, he is weeping bitterly.

He hardly hears the dull drumming and squelching of hoofs on the muddy cart track until they are close by him, and he only looks up when their rhythm ceases. Before him stands an old man, dressed in a filthy rust-coloured cloak and a felt hat, who regards him, head cocked to one side, dark eyes fixed upon him, with the expression of a quizzical parrot. The man turns to the two mares, which are heavily laden with bags, murmuring a quiet command to them. They stamp, snort, toss their heads, fall silent. Next his wishbone legs swing him to William's side, where he crouches with difficulty.

'In't the wind and rain enough,' he exclaims suddenly, 'without thy sighs and tearfulness!'

William smiles at once, for he remembers well the fat, rutted face – skin the colour and coarseness of sacking – which hovers six inches from his own, as that of the packman. This pedlar has been seen less frequently in the village each year, perhaps only once each spring and winter. As a consequence, his visits cause ever more excitement because of their rarity.

Those bulging packs contain exotic treasures – scented teas and strange confections, the finest lace and ribbons, the most aromatic tobacco, new broadsheets and ballads, and a hundred toys and trinkets. Hence the packman arrives like a visitor from another world (or more accurately, like a time traveller from the imminent future), bringing with him the latest news of wars, politics, fashion and customs from the new and alien cities. So strange and inconceivable are these tales told to the villagers, they can never decide whether this other world, advancing inexorably towards the close horizons of their own, should be thought of as a paradise or a hell.

'Never a day goes by,' the loquacious packman observes, 'without this poor pedlar finds some woeful creature weeping by the wayside. I've seen more tragical actors out in the world than a gentleman could ever see on the London stage. That's a fact. So what can ail so small a lad?'

William describes in a torrent of words the disappearance of his father and the fate which is about to befall him in the workhouse.

'A beatin' and a starvin' to death? That's a bad end for a mere lad!' the packman declares. 'Where's thy father then?'

William shakes his head and starts to cry. The packman frowns, rubbing his stubbly chin.

'He'll have gone down to Manchester. Most do, if they want for work or drink. The busier the place, the easier the pickings.'

'Then I'll go and find him there,' William announces, suddenly full of resolution. 'Which way is it?'

The packman pulls William to his feet.

'Better to walk with me, since I'll be making my way to there, or at least to some of the villages around. If you're set on going, meet me early tomorrow, down at the river. When I've sold these wares, I'll sleep in the tavern. I'll tell 'em a tale or two, if there's a pint in it for me.'

Then he returns to the restless mares, and leads them on to Hades.

Chapter Three

At first light William is sitting on the parapet of the bridge, shivering and peering into the mist, eagerly awaiting the spectral approach of the packman and his two mares. But two hours pass without a sign of the pedlar. Eventually William slumps, tired and defeated, against the wall. He has just fallen asleep when hoofs ring on the Roman bridge and the yawning packman, unshaven and red-nosed, comes at last.

'Never a day goes by,' he proclaims, 'without this poor pedlar finds some stray urchin by the wayside. Good morning to you!'

He delves into the recesses of his cloak and produces, with the flourish of a magician, two thick slices of bread, between which is sandwiched a generous cut of cold mutton. William chews greedily as he walks by the packman's side, listening to his inexhaustible chatter.

Slate-grey continents of cloud drift across the sky; the day darkens and the wind springs up, running in light and dark green swathes across the long moorland grass. A distant hill is momentarily lit up in a vast cylinder of sunlight, which flickers, then is extinguished. William's teeth chatter, and he cups his hands over his aching ears as a slanting edge of rain approaches, its first drops stinging his cheeks.

The track which they are following has risen

gradually out of the river valley, to join a cattle-droving road across the moorland. Their progress is slow throughout the morning, because the packman insists on engaging every passing wayfarer or shepherd in conversation. William endures these encounters with fortitude, ambling to and fro disconsolately, whilst feeling the cold and longing for the final fare-wells which will allow their journey to continue. In this way he discovers the packman to be the most verbose of men. For as the mood takes him he talks to William, to the horses, to every passer-by, and not to be left out, even to himself. Yet in William's eyes he is a delightful, if frustrating, travelling companion, a friend full of optimism, resourcefulness and generosity.

For lunch he produces bread, cheese and sweet jam from his packs, follows this with a tune on a penny whistle, then falls to lamenting the passing of his trade.

'In Manchester,' he says, chewing tobacco and spitting out its juice like black contempt, 'and every-where, for that matter, never a day goes by without the opening of some shop. Armies of shopkeepers spring up daily! Each one's a thief to your common man, with their dried sloe leaves and their 'orrible flitches of bacon. They'll be the end of my kind. I shall be the very last of the poor packmen. The likes of me will never be seen again on the lanes of England. That's a fact.'

As the afternoon passes, with William growing more and more exhausted in the face of wind and rain, and yet more numbed by the packman's unceasing conver-sation, he is relieved to be allowed to ride on one of the mares.

By evening their journey has brought them to a turnpike gate. Here an eternity passes as the packman good-naturedly disputes the toll charges, before they are allowed to pass on towards the grey amalgamation of the town of Oldham, over which the tall brick chimneys of the spinning mills are sending up giant feathers of black smoke.

In the narrow and foul-smelling lanes and courts, overshadowed by the mills, darkness brings a fall of fine powdery snow. The packman draws up the mares in front of an ancient three-storey house, on which hangs a cracked and peeling sign:

LOGINS FOR TRAVLERS – GOOD BEDS

The packman flings open the door and William follows him into an unlit passageway which leads to the doorway of a large room, with a long table and benches at its centre. It is lit only by a crackling fire at the far end.

Two rows of indistinct faces are turned towards the newcomers, but William is struck most forcibly by the stifling atmosphere of the room – a choking conspiracy of the blazing and fuming coal fire, the reek of eye-stinging tobacco, and the fetid odour of unclean bodies. There are one or two nods or grunts of recognition before the packman calls out loudly for service.

'Now let's be having a stately room for me and this lad, a decent fresh loaf and a leg of mutton, a servant to stable the beasts without, and a quart of ale this very second, for my tongue is dry and cracked as an old saddle!'

For several moments there is no sound but the spitting of the fire, and it seems the packman is to be granted none of his desires. But presently an old woman stirs from the fireside, her clogs scraping along the sawdust-strewn floor as she shuffles around the table towards them. When she draws close William sees the stained woollen dress and shawl, but most of all the sightless eyes, deadened by rheum, as thick as glue.

'Winter's 'ere, eh?' she whispers hoarsely. 'For if I don't mistake that big mouth, Jack the Pedlar's back again. Regular as a ticking clock.'

Then her voice rises to a sudden, fearsome shout: 'Catherine!'

Instantly, running footsteps come from above. They race down the stairs and into the passageway and a bare-footed girl of six or seven years appears, her face pale and her eyes bleary, framed by brown matted hair.

'Stablin' to be done,' the old woman tells her. 'Bring in the packs.'

'Aye, and keep thy greasy fingers out of 'em,' the packman adds, seizing the girl by the arm, 'or I'll see you don't sit down for a week.'

The girl slips out into the snow-deadened night.

'And so he says he's got a lad, does he?'

The old woman's hand gropes towards William.

'Come here, boy. Let's see what Jack's got himself.'

Her fingers find William's arm; she draws him close and bends down towards him. He is unable to hold her hideous gaze and pulls away, but she drags him back. Her face draws close to William's once more; stale breath envelops him. He begins to tremble as her fingers, calloused, filthy, with jagged nails, start to explore the shape of his face: first tracing the hollows of his eyes, then moving down the contours of his nose, finally following the curves of his lips. And still

27

these hands move down and around him, lingering on his buttocks, then delving between his legs.

'If thou'd not found him first,' she tells the packman, 'I'd let him lie upon me in a fit all night.'

Which sets off roars of black laughter from those around the table. Then the old woman shuffles back to her seat.

'Upstairs,' she announces. 'Any room, since none but Jack the Pedlar's foolish enough to be journeying in this weather.'

The packman takes a thin candle from the table, and leads the way up a winding staircase. He unlocks the door to a small room. William sees two mattresses, a broken wicker chair, rafters thick with old cobwebs, straw scattered on the floor. But an unshuttered window at least ensures that the air is fresh, though freezing; and those beds, though they are hard, uneven and badly infested, give promise of the great luxury of sleep.

The packman descends the stairs to fetch his bags which the girl has meanwhile dragged in from the street. William sits down on one of the beds whilst this task is accomplished, and cannot keep himself from yawning.

'Now are you to sleep, or drink with me?' the packman enquires. But William is already lying down, for memories of coarse, caressing hands and stale breath dissuade him from returning to the room downstairs.

'Then take this bag,' the packman continues, 'and sleep with your arms around it, as you would your brother or sister, for this is the town, and here never a day goes by without something criminal coming to pass. And another thing's for sure, that in the city of

Manchester it's far worse, for it grows like a monster.'

William is plunging into a deep sleep, and so is mercifully released from this universe of disturbing visions still being described by the packman long after William is beyond hearing – in the forms of dire poverty, overcrowding, rumours of revolution and plagues of typhus fever, which stalk this phantom city of Manchester. The city has sprawled into its suburbs of Salford and Chorlton, to provide the purgatorial home for over a quarter of a million souls. And this place, for which William is bound, now lies only a league away.

It is difficult to determine the precise manner in which the next twist of fate transforms the boy's life, although we can be certain of its outcome. My father is convinced that William's separation from the packman must be an imminent event, since he is to grow up in the Manchester area. In view of this, we must consider the circumstances in which William takes his leave of the man who is, at this very moment, tiptoeing from the room and stealthily bolting the door behind him, in that small, insalubrious lodging house in Oldham.

My father suggests to me that when confronted by such a problem, it is most fitting to consider the very best and the very worst version of events. I reply that, in such a world, we had better put our faith in the worst.

William feels a prodding in his ribs, murmurs and tries to stay asleep. The next moment his shoulder is being shaken roughly and he opens his eyes. How long has he slept? No insipid light of dawn seeps through the tiny window of the room; only a candle flame wavers in the darkness. Then William rolls over to a nightmarish awakening, for the spectral figure of the packman is standing over him. At first he can make no sense of this confused image – a face he hardly recognizes, staring down at him over a huge expanse of belly. And yet the hand at his groin cups an unmistakable offering.

'Touch me,' whispers the packman, and William smells the ale on his breath.

'Once done, thou'll never live without it.'

William stares in bewilderment into the packman's eyes, but his expression of benevolence has vanished utterly, now that his subtle abduction of the boy has come to the point of fruition.

'Touch me, else I'll strangle thee!' hisses the packman, thrusting himself forward. But William is gone like a frightened hare in one spring from the bed, and is dashing for the door. The packman wheels, clutches the boy's shoulder, but he squirms and is loose again, tearing at the door handle. As the packman's arms enfold him he struggles furiously, and striking backwards with all his might, lands the blow that will save his life.

Now the packman gasps in agony and sinks to his knees, whilst William flies down the narrow staircase. He stumbles along the reeking passageway, tripping in the darkness over something which groans and grasps his ankle. He kicks himself free and immediately crashes into a closed door. His fingers find the latch, and no bolts prevent him from reaching the courtyard beyond.

William emerges into a world transformed beyond all recognition. The snow lies thick from the night's fall. It has cast its white disguise and its terrifying silence all around. The shock of this brings William skidding to a stop; he can neither remember the route by which he came to this place, nor can he guess which alleys will be blind, or will carry him to freedom.

So time misses a beat; a horse splutters behind a stable door; from the loft above comes the fluttering of hens' wings. The courtyard is deserted; black windows stare down; steep roofs are fringed with snow. The sky bears down, like a huge grey millstone.

Then the panic which clutches at William makes time begin again. Whether they exist or not, he hears pursuing footsteps and is gone, running on the treacherous snow, which drains him of strength and deprives him of speed. He emerges from the alleyway into a street where already crowds of men, women and children are swarming to the mills to begin their day's work.

Only when he is almost a mile from the town and houses have given way to deserted fields does he feel safe enough to collapse on to a bank, to regain his breath. From this vantage point he can see that he is not being followed, but still he watches anxiously, whilst the town begins to assume its forbidding form in the dismal light of dawn. The chimneys send up their first plumes of smoke in their daily conspiracy to shroud the town in fog. As the morning progresses the greyness will gather, until in every street and alleyway black soot will rain upon the snow which begins to fall gently once more, soaking the still-damp clothes in which William has slept. He crouches in the shelter of a stone wall, his teeth chattering, and continues to survey the road behind him until he is certain that no-one is pursuing him. Then he sets off at a steady trot, throwing frequent glances over his shoulder.

After covering nearly four miles in this way he reaches the settlement of Ashton-under-Lyne. Yet he does not linger here, for he fears that this place will also be the packman's next destination. At length the road he chooses brings him to a small town of some six thousand inhabitants: Denton.

Outside the Red Lion inn, a crowd has gathered to watch a pavement dentist at work. A frail old man, the unfortunate owner of a rotten tooth, is seated on a chair. His one defence against the coming agony has been provided by a large measure of gin. The dentist, massive and bearded, in a bloodstained white apron suitable for a butcher, instructs three burly fellows to force the old man down into his seat. Then, in a lightning movement, he produces a pair of pliers from his pocket. His left hand forces open the old man's jaws; his right hand plunges the instrument within, secures a hold, and with a fearful, twisting wrench, and a massive grunt of exertion, rips the offending tooth from its socket.

The old man, half-drunk and numb with terror, moans feebly and lurches forward, a gout of blood on his chin, which drips on to the melting snow. But he is quite forgotten by the crowd as the dentist holds up the yellow and twisted prize, still clutched in the jaws of the pliers, and graciously accepts the applause of the spectators.

The crowd drifts away, and William wanders on aimlessly. His confidence, both in his direction and in his ability to find his father, begins to wane; the visions

32

created by the packman of a colossal and Babylonian metropolis return to haunt him.

He opens the gate to Denton Old Church and sits down against the graveyard wall. All at once his misery and fear find expression in a torrent of tears. When the service ends on this particular Sunday morning and the members of the congregation depart, to return to their drawing rooms into which the smell of roasted joints is already wafting, they pass by the spectacle of a ragged boy. He is huddled in the snow, too exhausted to care who sees him there.

The theme of that morning's sermon – the need for Christian charity – is instantly forgotten by several worshippers who speculate on the benefits to the nation, should street urchins be made to spend Sunday mornings within a church, rather than without it.

One person stops, however, as the crowd files through the gate. William thus finds himself to be the object of the concerned if somewhat stern scrutiny of Joseph Mallory.

Chapter Four

'And why must you go to Manchester?' he asks.

It is his ninth question in succession. Joseph Mallory's mind is of an interrogative cast. He is both a product of the time in which he exists and, in a small way, a creator of it. He yearns to understand the workings of phenomena – whether they are machines or experiences makes no difference – and so he spends his life dismantling and reassembling them, in order to discover their essential qualities. In that face, with its restless eyes, its forehead lined with concentration, there is the stamp of impatience: impatience for an age of discovery to come to fruition, and the forces of a new industrial spirit to shape the world's progress.

From where I now sit at my father's desk I can glance up at the notice board, to see a photograph of Joseph Mallory in later life, which my father somehow unearthed in his research. The dark hair has thinned out, the black whiskers have turned grey, the face is furrowed with a lifetime of seeking. Yet the eyes now betray not so much an expression of impatience as one of perplexity, of more important questions unanswered, of some metaphysical disappointment.

But as he stands by the gate of Denton Old Church, becoming increasingly moved by the plight of William

Daniels, his dreams, of which we shall learn more, are still in their relative infancy.

Perhaps it is the mention of Hades (a village which Joseph knows well, since his own birthplace was not far from there); or the timely theme of the morning's sermon – or a combination of both – which persuades him to practise what has just been preached at him.

But it is no easy matter to satisfy William that this stranger intends no harm, and his offers of charity are greeted initially with alarm and suspicion. However, in the end, William must accept that he is engaged in an unequal struggle, for he is weary, cold and hungry, and even to his wary eyes Joseph Mallory undoubtedly speaks and dresses as a gentleman. He realizes that he is at risk if he chooses to accept Joseph Mallory's entreaties, but he has no alternative. So they set off together.

Nearly a mile from the gate of the church lies the farm to which Joseph Mallory came as owner in 1829, and adjacent to this stands a row of workshops with a painted sign above the door: J. MALLORY & CO. – HAT MAKERS.

William is forced to bathe in a hot tub; his skin is scrubbed to pink brightness by Joseph Mallory, who wields without mercy a stiff scrubbing brush and a large cake of soap. So that it is a somewhat disgruntled, yet cleanly and shaven-headed boy who is invited to enjoy the first full roast dinner of his life in the farmhouse kitchen, and to retire afterwards to a clean and comfortable bed in the attic room of the farmhouse. Still he lies awake all night, dreading a footstep on the stairs, a rattle of the door handle; but his fears prove unfounded. On the following morning he is roused for breakfast, then is set to work, helping on the farm and in the workshop, where coarse felts are being made from rabbit furs.

Joseph Mallory is quick to see that William applies himself industriously to any task allotted to him. In his new protector's mind a plan is slowly taking shape for William's future. He will, of course, make enquiries in the appropriate places concerning the whereabouts of the missing father. Should Bartholomew Daniels be found in the phantom city of his son's imagination, the boy will be entrusted to him, so long as the father proves himself to be morally wholesome; should he fail to do so, Joseph will teach William the art of making hats.

This intended apprenticeship springs, however, not from purely philanthropic motives, but also from deeper impulses. Two years previously Joseph's wife died in giving birth to a son, who outlived her for only three hours. William will make tangible the ghostly presence of the lost child, who runs round the silent, lifeless rooms of the farmhouse, chattering and laughing. He will go hand in hand with the boy who lies in Denton churchyard, yet who still exists, growing up in Joseph Mallory's imagination.

Furthermore, the owner of the hat-making firm has been determined to expand his business, to bring together all the manufacturing processes under one roof, which will be supported by the walls of a brand-new factory that has already risen from the ground in his entrepreneurial fancy. So, as the days pass, Joseph clings ever more fiercely to an idea: he envisages a future in which he is a rich old man, able to retire to his books and his studies, whilst William skilfully and loyally administers the business.

Meanwhile these first days of freedom open up a

new universe of sensations for William. He squints through a telescope for the first time, to see the moon adjusted from a vague, milky blob to a sharply defined image of a luminous disc, its surface grainy and pitted. At break of day each morning he climbs to the hayloft of the ancient barn. Where slates have slipped to admit columns of dusty, pale lemon light, these seem to support the roof above him. He steps between them, stealthily gathering a hoard of white and speckled eggs, the silence only disturbed by the fluttering of hidden wings in the shadows. And in the evenings he sits in a rocking chair by a spitting log fire, whilst his mentor patiently encourages his mind into literate and numerate modes of thinking.

So William's young existence has been infused with unexpected promise. There is nothing we can do, on the other hand, to prolong the life of Bartholomew Daniels beyond middle age. He will survive for five years more in the city of Manchester, inviting the desolate end which awaits him in the winter of 1841. It is something of a triumph that he endures this long, for he is starved of nourishing food and poisoned by cheap gin, the money for which he acquires by begging or by stealing. No-one can rescue him from the foul-smelling streets of Little Ireland, where he sleeps at night in the dank and populous cellars of crumbling tenements. Until it proves to be futile, Joseph Mallory advertises periodically for information concerning Bartholomew's whereabouts. But the ruined man cannot afford to purchase newspapers, which are in any case of no use to him since he is illiterate, nor has he contact with any person with the ability to read. His life and his individuality subside into the cesspit which is the world of Little Ireland – one of indignity and futility, of criminality, and mental and physical illness – a world which, in a short time to come, will fall under the appalled scrutiny of Friedrich Engels.

So – unaware that he once was sought for his son's sake – he is brought, insane and ranting, in the final stages of delirium tremens, to the crowded cellar of a workhouse. Here, on the eve of the New Year of 1842, he is beaten to death by an Irish prizefighter, whose pocket he foolishly and unsuccessfully tries to pick.

William's fate was sealed, of course, long before this day. When the new factory began to rise from real and solid foundations, he was apprenticed into hat-making and he diligently mastered the intricacies of the new machinery.

To prove how effectively he did so, it will suffice to state that, by the age of twenty – in 1845 – William was appointed as Joseph Mallory's assistant factory manager.

The combination of Joseph Mallory's loyalty to his protégé and William Daniels's diligence in his duties to his patron had proved an unbreakable bond. This endured throughout the depression which stultified the hat-making industry during the early 1840s, bringing a strike in 1841 and a fall in wages of one-third during that period. Joseph delegated more and more power to the younger man.

In 1843, at the age of eighteen, William married Elizabeth White, the daughter of an inventor of hatting machinery, and a child, Mary, was born to them in 1844. When William became Joseph Mallory's deputy he was able to rent a cottage for his family, close to the works, and then began to make plans for the day when he would set up his own hatting business.

William has been saved by the coming of the machine age by the very phenomenon which ruined his father. But his happiness is to be short-lived, and the machine age is to prove an untrustworthy ally. Fourteen fortunate years end for William on a spring morning in 1849, when a new, but flawed, factory boiler explodes, atomizing him, decapitating another worker (it was reported that this man ran headless amidst the ruins), and maiming three others.

After William's scant remains are laid to rest in the churchyard to which he first came as a ragged boy, Joseph Mallory – without the heart and the energy to salvage his dreams – sells his devastated factory. He becomes once more the recluse, falling back into the solitariness from which the arrival of William had reclaimed him.

Elizabeth has a little money left to her by her husband with which to support herself and her child. They live on in the small cottage, which grows ever more dilapidated, in the aftermath of the 'Hungry Forties'. And each morning she gazes from her cottage window towards the factory, which still resounds in her mind with that deafening catastrophe.

After Joseph Mallory's death irreversible poverty sets in; for Elizabeth no longer enjoys the protection of the man who loved her husband as his own son. And in any case, the old man's dream of wealth has proved unfounded, his debts on machinery more burdensome than he realized, the pinch of the 'Hungry Forties' more financially bruising after that decade had closed.

Elizabeth finds paid labour as a seamstress, but the

exodus from the countryside to the multiplying towns makes work scarce. Perhaps we should not be too harsh on the widow for treating her growing daughter with severity. Her own frustrations have grown, too. She finds herself beset by poverty, by long and tedious hours of needlework, or worse still, by empty hours of anxiety, when she is unable to earn any money at all. All this is compounded by the invidious pity showered upon her by her neighbours.

Mary is constantly scolded by her mother, for she is a constant reminder of a great tragedy. Nor should we be surprised to discover that the daughter grows up to believe that her mother hates her, and secretly returns that hatred with interest. In the twisted logic of emotions, Mary comes to blame her mother for wilfully depriving her of a father.

Mary begins to run away from home. At first only for an hour or so, until her mother's anger subsides. We see her returning to the factory where her father perished – against her mother's express instructions – to watch the men in the workshops. The dim interior reveals to her bowler-hatted labourers attired in tail-coats, black trousers and shining clogs, industriously engaged in the dipping and rolling out of conical pieces of rough material; reveals the gleaming copper drying cabinets, which house the hat blocks for stretching the felts; and beyond, reveals the huge, malignant boilers, wheezing and gasping in the steamy air, impregnated with a pungent odour of lacquer.

And eventually Mary is displaced to the extremes of her mother's affections, when the foreman of the business which has newly established itself at the factory begins to pay an increasing heed to Elizabeth's welfare. As a part of this welfare Mary is left alone for many interminable evenings, whilst her mother and her new companion take themselves off to public houses, returning at late hours with an accompaniment of giggles, slaps, urgent whispers, creaking stairs, and stifled moans of some unknown pleasure or pain, enacted in the adjacent bedroom. Such sounds, which permeate the night, filter into Mary's uncomprehending heart until it is bursting with cold terror and despair.

She begins to flee the house for whole mornings or afternoons, thus incurring even greater wrath when she returns. And so, in the end, she decides to run away for ever.

Chapter Five

Witness again my father at work, engrossed in some obscure nineteenth-century publication – his head bowed, spectacles perched precariously on the end of his aquiline nose.

His professional life is over; he has left behind the stifling air of the staff-room, the grey flagstones of the colonnaded quadrangle, the oak-panelled corridors which will smell for eternity of beeswax and bleach; has hung up the inky gown, powdered with random patterns of chalk dust – like zodiacs on a night of black perfection – for the last time; has swapped the mortarboard of the professional teacher of history for the cap of the amateur genealogist.

It is all for the best: he has seen an establishment which exclusively educated young gentlemen, over a history of five hundred years, throw open its gates to an invasion of young women. He has seen traditions which have endured for half a millennium crumble in the space of months. I tell him it is inevitable, irresistible, and all for the best. He is not an intolerant man; he has simply grown too old, for too long in the same fashion, to take change and adjustment in his stride.

Now he has become an amateur genealogist. It is a lonely undertaking, though many feel compelled to rise to its challenges. They set forth into a forest of difficulties, ill-equipped, with inadequate provisions, knowing only their starting point. They hope, vainly, to map out a baffling network of tracks, long since overgrown. But once begun, their task becomes ever more obsessional, the more it seems impossible. Some are quickly defeated: the past throws up a sheer, unscalable cliff face, so that they will never set eyes upon the promised land beyond it; others, often by a stroke of sheer good luck, penetrate further into the twisting labyrinth of history.

And so my father has become a victim of this fascination, blinded to the fact that others can be exhausted by his fervour. He is a bore – albeit a forgivable one, for his fanaticism harms nobody – who can send yawns around a dinner table faster than the port, by relating, for example, at great length how the Mormons of Salt Lake City house their genealogical records underground, in missile-proof shelters. 'How paradoxical,' he will exclaim to his rapt audience, 'that at humanity's end, *genealogy*, of all things, should survive!'

My father is one of those distracted ghosts which you sometimes see in country churchyards, making notes of grave inscriptions or staring for long periods at the horizon, where you can see nothing, but he sees villages and tribes of people going about their business. He passes hours, along with others touched by this malady of the brain, in the waiting rooms of St Catherine's House, or the Public Record Office at Kew, or in any number of musty archives, in expectation of a glimpse at some dusty yellowing decayed sheaf of papers, some abstruse will, or convoluted testament.

And then, in his study, he will create diagrammatical representations of progeny, blocked out on the

43

page like the façade of a pyramid. He dreams of passenger lists for steam and sailing ships, of coats of arms, of bastard offspring and incestuous relations, of excommunications and transportations, of patricide, matricide, fratricide, sororicide, infanticide and suicide. But in all his work he must be patient, resourceful, diligent and thorough. And in these things my father has not failed himself.

He is to be applauded for the discoveries he has made: he has stood on a rainswept hillside, amidst the ruins of the village of Hades, and has surveyed the acres of land where a small boy named William Daniels ran over the ploughed earth, waving his arms and whooping at the top of his voice to scare away the crows. And he has stood in the shadows of the walls of Joseph Mallory's hat-making factory, where the roof has caved in, but the factory chimney still stands.

He can tell you how the factory survived under new ownership into this century, until its export trade was strangled by the coming of the Second World War. And how it was too late after that, for the fashion for wearing hats was dead and both men and women could walk the streets of Denton bare-headed; whereas a mere decade before, when hat-making was the lifeblood of the town, such behaviour would have appeared so outrageous as to have been of near-criminal proportions.

No, my father has not failed himself in his work, despite the fact that certain faculties of his are failing him in theirs. His eyes are failing, so that tiny print and elaborate handwriting strain his vision. And his heart is murmuring in the protest that sixty-eight years is a considerable time to have been beating steadily. He no longer ventures far from home, and so requires the assistance of my mother and myself (when I visit them), to fetch or photocopy documents for him, and to guide him through mazes of difficult print.

He knows that the end of his future is a horizon moving inexorably closer, hour by hour, day by day; and so his eyes are fixed firmly on the past. But it is a curious process by which he must start from the present and tunnel back into the past, in order to understand something of the way forward.

So those days are past when my father would suggest, on the spur of the moment, an expedition during the long school vacations, and we would set off in the Triumph Herald (my mother having no spirit for such occasions), armed with maps, books, photographs and a few clothes. More often than not our destination would be Penzance, and – if we avoided the busiest holiday periods – we would have few difficulties in securing rooms in a sea-front hotel for two or three nights.

At that time my father had come into possession of two key clues to the mystery which he wished to unravel, but he was far from determining their significance, and far from fitting them into a coherent narrative . . .

Early one Sunday morning we took a stroll along the promenade from Penzance to Newlyn, then turned up the Coombe, beside which a small but vigorous stream flows. We were looking for what my father called 'locations', as if we had a half-formed storyline for a film, into which we had to build real people and real places in order to achieve verisimilitude.

We stopped as we came to a large stone-built house,

set back from the lane. A long garden path separated a croquet lawn from well-tended flowerbeds. We continued a little further up the lane to survey the house from its side aspect, and then we noticed that there was a conservatory at the rear. This set off a train of thought in my father's head.

'That's *exactly* as I see the house, Tom ... Yes, because of the conservatory, of course. North-facing, perfect for his purposes.'

I nodded, threw in a question here and there. I had, in fact, only half-listened to my father's theories and speculations during the long drive down from London. My adolescent mind had been magnetized in other directions, namely girls, pop music and poetry, for I had already – or so I liked to think – become a writer in earnest.

And so I was only mildly interested in those complex riddles which engaged my father. Only now, as they fade in the suffusing glow of nostalgia, do I attach any importance to these scenes.

We climbed over a low wall and ascended a hillside. There was a copse of trees by which we halted and sat down, my father breathing heavily. I could sense his excitement as he nodded and muttered to himself, contemplating the back of the house and its conservatory. It seemed as though he knew he was tantalizingly close to a revelation. But then he stood up abruptly, still effectively addressing himself.

'Yes, this certainly bears some thinking about. Only a hunch, of course . . . needs a lot more research, son.'

So he set off, head bowed, hands thrust deep into the pockets of his shapeless tweed jacket, unlit pipe protruding from his lips, his brow scored by an agonizing frown.

We walked back along the Penzance promenade, all the way to the harbour, whilst my father lamented the desecration wrought by 'fish'n'chips' and souvenir shops: 'Because,' he emphasized, 'I know *exactly* how this promenade looked one hundred years ago.'

Yet out of its vile modernity came visions to torment me: beautiful, radiant, semi-clad girls of my own age drifted by, their limbs browned by the sun, their hair flowing in the sea breezes – visions which filled me with some unnameable, unbearable longing.

At the harbour my father paused, gazing intently out to sea, lost in thought. Eventually he seemed to sense my growing frustration, for he patted me on the shoulder and with a sly wink enquired whether I was in need of some refreshment. Whereupon he led me into the Dolphin tavern and provided me with a pint of best bitter, despite my being under age by fourteen months: such was my reward for patiently humouring his indulgences.

Chapter Six

On a summer evening in 1855 a dozen brightly-painted caravans arrive at Denton Common. Each wagon bears the legend DAY'S EXTRAORDINARY TRAVELLING CIRCUS. Once Mary learns of its coming she begins to haunt the fairground, excited by its atmosphere of revelry and mystery, and by the high spirits of the crowds which are drawn there.

Now conjure up the sideshow entitled DAY'S EXHIBITION OF CURIOSITIES. A wooden hall has been constructed with a door in its front wall; on each of the panels of the façade renderings of the Curiosities have been depicted by an artist of questionable genius. In one of these crudely stylized paintings a man with the head of a monkey stands beside a diminutive goat-faced child. Beyond these a darkened cage is represented, wherein a host of deformed and pitiable creatures is imprisoned.

On either side of the door, on a raised platform, two men stand as forbidding sentinels. Dressed identically in white shirts, black bow-ties and waistcoats and tall black hats, each of these moustachioed waxwork figures leans on a large painting. One shows a grossly overweight woman; the other a dwarf in the costume of an Elizabethan pageboy.

Between these grim effigies stands Matthew Day himself, whose own living appearance presents something of a curiosity to the eye, with his thin stooped frame, mottled skin and straggling whiskers, his battered top hat and threadbare, mildewed frock-coat.

He is regaling a small audience with descriptions of the wonders and horrors which lie beyond the door of the Exhibition, casting his eyes voraciously across the rows of upturned faces. And yet after a few moments he seems to falter in his well-rehearsed speech. His gaze no longer sweeps the crowd, but lingers on Mary's face, then darts away, only to return seconds later.

Despite the lack of conviction in his delivery, two or three people are nevertheless persuaded to venture inside the Exhibition. Matthew Day hurriedly takes their money and ushers them through the door. But he does not follow them into the gloom; instead, he bounds down the steps of the platform in a surprisingly agile fashion and plants himself before Mary, bending down and staring intently into her eyes. She feels suddenly afraid but he grasps her by the arm, drawing her close to him and enveloping her in odours of stale sweat and tobacco, a pellet of which he unexpectedly ejects with great force over her shoulder, from between his scaly lips.

'No, stay. Let me see that face.'

He scrutinizes her, at uncomfortably close quarters, then shakes his head in wonderment.

'Good Lord,' he murmurs. 'It's a miracle.'

Day leads Mary by the hand, away from the fair, to a caravan which stands on its own, dragging her up the stairs to the door, which he throws open. No candles burn within, and Mary's first impression is of the warm perfumed darkness of its interior. As she stands on the threshold, she sees first of all a line of faces

49

come to life on the opposite wall – disembodied heads, hanging as if on invisible gallows, their expressions set in masks of grotesque tragedy or maniacal comedy.

Next, three low beds and a square table emerge from their shadowy existences. The table is crowded with bottles and jars, each bearing a handwritten label which describes the elixir therein: 'Day's Extraordinary Unction For The Banishment Of Melancholy – Apply to the Suffering Brow with Poultices'; 'Day's Magikal Curative For The Trew Easement of Gout'; 'Day's Mirakulous Oyntment For The Soothing Of Boyles, Rashes, Bunyons, Stiffen'd Joynts, Fevers & The General Healthe Of The Bodie & Soule – Very Medicinal'.

Crooked shelves hold the mundane ingredients of these astonishing potions. They support a good many baskets of dried herbs and flower petals, pots of mud, rows of jars which contain the murky distillations of boiled fruits. An enormous wooden bowl represents the crucible, and a sturdy pestle the magic wand, by which Matthew Day transmutes these base elements into medicinal gold.

'Wake up!' exclaims Day, shaking something which lies under a blanket on a bed.

A girl sits up with a groan of fatigue.

'Get up! There's a good girl! I wish you to become h'acquainted with a young friend of mine.'

Day lights a candle; the interior of the caravan jolts itself into reality; and the girl casts back her cover, rising unsteadily to her feet. Light leaps to her face. Then each girl studies the image of her double.

'They say all children are alike. But you two children are *very* alike, as to be almost h'indistinguishable, one from the other. Why, as I stood on my platform, I totally mistook you, one for the other. What's your name then?'

'Mary,' Mary whispers.

'And this one here is my own flesh and blood, known by the name of Katy. Now, what with you being like twin sisters, has put me in mind of an idea – a most subtell idea.'

Day plucks at his scanty beard.

'Naturally, as to all subtell ideas, there remains an h'obstacle. Such as the ties of blood, as what ties me to my child here, her mother having been taken from us. So say, what may be your ties, Mary? Where is the binding of flesh and blood, in the forms of your dear father and mother?'

Mary does not answer, but glances bewilderedly between the faces of the father and daughter, and along the line of grinning and weeping paper masks. She takes a step backwards.

'No, no. Don't be afraid,' says Day with a sudden tenderness in his voice. 'After all, you came to my fair, quite on your own, I think. So you cannot be so affeared. But is your father nearby?'

Mary replies that he is not.

'Is he anywhere in the wide world?'

Mary considers this for a while, then shakes her head.

'Well then,' says Matthew Day, nodding his head and scratching more violently at his sparse beard. 'I h'often think how regrettable it is that fathers and mothers are too keen to die, or run away, leaving their poor offspring to fend for themselves. Yet at least it means there is no h'obstacle to my subtell idea – if only I can make it appeal to you.'

And the mildewed arms of his frock-coat snake

around the girls' shoulders, drawing them together, face to face, like a figure pressed against a mirror.

Some weeks later the 'Exhibition of Curiosities' materializes in a suburb of Birmingham, where it is able to boast an attraction hitherto unwitnessed. People pay their money and pass through the curtains to peer into a row of cramped and ill-lit cages, in which they are afforded the spectacles of The Black Dwarf and The World's Fattest Woman. Their eyes also alight, with varying expressions of compassion and scepticism, upon another unnatural sight – the heads of two small girls, which protrude through a hole in a sheet. These identical twins sit or stand, or revolve back to back, as one living thing.

For, as Matthew Day proclaims from the platform: 'They have been from birth conjoined, condemned to share one backbone, which is both a Tragedy and a Miracle of Nature. So that One can never depart from the Other; for which means Almighty God has blessed them, by ensuring that they possess no Divisible Will, but speak and act with ultimate Accord and Harmony.'

Chapter Seven

It is a burning late-August day in 1945. The man who wears a cheap linen suit, carries a bulging rucksack and is trudging along a narrow lane sunk deep between sturdy hedges and steep banks, where long grass and wild flowers entwine, must live for another decade to become my father.

The lane meanders through the Cheshire countryside then begins to rise up, following the sweep of an isolated hill, and with the effort of climbing my father feels as if he is struggling along the sea bed of a boiling ocean. He prises the straps of the rucksack from his shoulders, throws his burden aside, and sinks down wearily on to a narrow shelf of shadow at the foot of the hedge. He remains there for several minutes, breathing fitfully, his body half in cool shade, half in scathing light, exhausted yet entranced by the stillness, the intoxicating scents at the lane's verge and the phrases of birds concealed in the thicket.

He contemplates the unbroken powder-blue of the sky, which has regained its ancient peace, free at last from the screaming of Spitfires, the droning of Lancasters, the spluttering of flying bombs.

My father has spent nine months in the confines of hospitals and convalescent homes; and even now he has not fully regained the strength of his legs and back. After eternities of communal refectories and dormitories, he wallows in the acute bliss of solitariness. There is no other traveller on the lane to distract him from his reveries, and no vehicles pass him, so he lies supine, lost deep in his remembrances.

For the first time in many months he feels emotionally becalmed, as if he has reached the equator of his recent past, from which the recollections of a man who is dead and a woman who is alive can recede to distant, opposite poles – too remote from him to matter. Perhaps I have broken free at last, he thinks, from the grief and the longing. But after a while this imaginary world collapses, and he becomes again the point towards which the past inexorably implodes.

So he rouses himself, cursing and weeping, straps on the rucksack and continues along the lane. In due course the house of Elias Crane, his father, appears before him, half-hidden by a copse of poplar trees. It is an ancient thatched farmhouse, the oldest part of which dates from the Jacobean period. Now several decades have passed since its façade was last whitewashed, and it is stained and flaking, so that a dark skeleton of oak beams has become apparent around the windows and the low door.

My father enters the long garden by the gate at the end of a footpath. Dusk is falling, draining the tired colours from its chaotic tangle of wild roses, foxgloves and lupins. Two exotic trees, their black boughs strangely contorted, stand on either side of the path.

He opens the door and steps into a cool dim hallway, gratefully casting off his rucksack. Silence. But the silence does not accord with memory. The missing element is the ticking of a towering grandfather clock, the clock which – as his mother always told him – 'was ticking during the French Revolution'. The clock still stands in its alcove, but it has been struck dumb. Upon its ornate face the phases of golden suns and silver moons have stopped in their tracks. My father passes on into the drawing-room.

This low but spacious room once boasted a highly polished wooden floor, but its sheen has long since vanished under a thick veneer of compounded dust. The ceiling is traversed by great blackened beams, and the white plaster of the walls has surrendered to a swarm of soot, for the deep fireplace with its high carved surround has come to dominate the room in more ways than one. A large discoloured oil painting of a beach scene hangs above the fireplace. Before it are ranged a chaise longue, its crimson velvet worn smooth and metallic in appearance, and two old leather armchairs out of which the horsehair has exploded here and there, creating shapes like strange fungi on the dead branches of a tree. An old upright piano, surmounted by a huge valve-driven radio, complete the furniture of the room. A number of potted plants stand upon the windowsill, but all are withered and netted by spiders' webs. The air in the room is acrid, as though it has not been changed for a hundred years.

Through an open door, which leads into a small book-lined study, my father sees his father, sitting at a desk, engrossed in a folder which lies open before him.

'Hello, Father,' he says.

There is a long silence. My grandfather looks up, blinks, as though he is emerging from a deep dream. His expression is one of cold recognition.

'Well . . . have you won the war?'

'Not personally . . . But the war is won.'

My father sinks wearily into a leather armchair.

'Surely you must have heard . . .' he continues after a few moments.

His father seems confused.

'The radio . . .' And he gestures towards the squat contraption housed in Bakelite. 'Broken.'

'And the clock's stopped.'

'I have no need of the time. Why are you here?' he adds.

'Because of what I wrote in my letter to you. Don't you remember?'

'Mmm . . . I have some vague recollection of a letter . . .'

Father and son lapse into silence. At length my father speaks.

'The house . . . it seems there's work to do.'

'Does it? Perhaps you are right.'

Then Elias Crane returns his attention to the papers on his desk.

My father takes up residence in the attic room where he slept throughout his childhood and adolescence, and enters into a strange, wordless relationship with his father.

On fine days my grandfather rises early, gathers together a box of paints, brushes, canvas and easel and sets out into the fields, with the apparent intention of producing landscapes. Yet when he returns each afternoon his intentions appear to have yielded nothing of significance in terms of creativity. And he shows total reluctance to display these meagre results to his son. My father is reduced to sneaking into the study to view the work after Elias has retired for the night. It is always the same; the canvases bear witness to only a few random brush strokes.

Intrigued by this, my father's curiosity drives him, on one occasion, to follow his father into the fields, to watch as the old man meticulously sets up the easel, arranges paints on the palette, then proceeds to do nothing except to stare intently at the blank canvas, or at the horizon, over which pours the changing light of the day, bringing its shifting moods to earth and sky.

My father finds such behaviour inexplicable; that someone should prepare himself so thoroughly for an activity, then produce nothing, seems alien to his practical mind. Better to paint badly after making such careful preparations, would be his maxim, than not to paint at all.

So as a psychological antidote to the old man's behaviour, my father becomes determined that he will prove the point. He pedals to the village on a rusty bicycle with flat tyres, locates the nearest source of whitewash, haggles over the price, buys a large quantity and conveys it back to the farmhouse, by way of several trips with loaded panniers. Then he sets to work in earnest, to renovate the paintwork.

From morning to night he stands on a ladder, his insteps aching, the muscles of his arms and his back constricted with pain, naked from the waist upwards in the dream-inducing heat of those summer days. Yet he drives himself mercilessly, out of some vague sense of outrage, some grim resolution, as if he is enacting a moral lesson for his father's benefit. But it is all in vain, for his father seems oblivious to his industrious example.

At length the exterior of the farmhouse is completed, and my father sets to work indoors. On hands and knees he scrapes the wooden floor of the drawing room, sandpapers the surface and lays coats of lustrous varnish. He dusts, polishes, disposes of dead plants, stuffs the horsehair back into the leather armchairs and patches up the cracks. His father goes about his indeterminate business and the two men only meet over dinner. My father invariably prepares this meal, the eating of which is accompanied by little or no conversation.

Then one day Elias surprises his son, as the latter is cleaning the oil painting which hangs above the fireplace. My father has taken a bowl of soapy water and is applying wads of soaked cotton wool to the painted surface.

'Leave that alone,' Elias tells him.

'But it's filthy, Father. This is the correct way to clean it. I assure you it won't cause damage.'

Elias moves away to his study door, then turns to regard his son with a look of pure contempt.

'Are you intending to stay here for ever? Why can't you find yourself a job and leave me in peace!'

And then he is gone, slamming the door after him.

From that moment my father abandons all attempts to renovate the property, or to make the household run smoothly. He stays in his attic room, writing letters and keeping a journal, which can only be a depository for anger, or self-pity, in view of his hopeless predicament. He walks desultorily along lanes and across fields, heedless of his surroundings, or cycles to the village to pick up newspapers from the post office and to make telephone calls. There is no escape in sleep, for sleep brings terrible nightmares.

Weeks and months pass by in this way, whilst autumn inveigles itself into sky and land. Elias no longer attempts to paint outdoors, but keeps himself shut up in his bedroom or study. On my father's dressing table the letters of rejection accumulate, until the morning when he receives the almost shocking news that 'owing to a withdrawal of acceptance of the chosen candidate' he is to be offered a job as a junior master of history at a school in south London, subject to a satisfactory interview.

He imparts this information to his father at once.

'Oh dear,' comes the response, 'must you leave soon?'

My father regrets that he must, but indicates that he may have some initial expenses to cover.

Elias appears to absorb this information, then to dismiss it instantly from his mind, for he finds a screwdriver with which he slowly sets about removing the back panel from the radio. He gropes inside the casing and produces a bundle of notes, which he offers to his son.

'You must write,' he says. 'I seem to remember that I enjoy your letters.'

My father is gone within the hour, with the rising of two expectations: that he is to begin a career, and that he will meet again the woman with whom he has fallen in love.

For she has replied at long last to his letters, which he addressed to the convalescent home where he was confined at the end of the war. He was not to know that she had ceased her voluntary work there not long after his departure, so that his correspondence was redirected several times before it finally fell into her hands.

Chapter Eight

To the end of his life, my father suffered from nightmares . . .

One Saturday morning, when I was not long past my sixteenth birthday, and was enjoying a common delusion of adolescence – that I had reached intellectual maturity and, as a result, the world and the values of the previous generation in particular were worthy of nothing but my scorn and contempt – I found a letter on the doormat which was addressed to my father, and which bore the CND symbol.

I tossed the envelope on to my father's desk, at which he was marking books, then assumed my most goading tone.

'Oh dear. The Commies want some money off you, Dad. Fat chance.'

I turned on my heels and made for the door. But I was arrested by a tremendous crash, as my father's fist came into contact with the desktop. I turned round, alarmed – for my father was always slow to anger – to see him rise to his feet, with an expression of fury on his face.

'Wrong on two counts! They are neither Communists, nor do they want money off me, since I already pay a subscription.'

'Don't make me laugh!'

He took a deep breath and closed his eyes, letting his anger subside to exasperation. We were back in the classroom: he the master at the end of his tether; I the witless pupil.

'So,' he began, 'my radical son doesn't suppose his reactionary father could have the intelligence to be terrified of the prospect of nuclear war. Is that it?'

I shrugged my shoulders, hoping also to shrug off my growing embarrassment.

'No . . . I merely assumed that CND was . . . alien to your way of life.'

He grimaced.

'War isn't *alien* to anyone's way of life, Tom. As a reality, it may not mean much to a sixteen-year-old English schoolboy, but the threat remains and it's increasing every day, so you'd be advised to start treating it with a little seriousness.'

'You don't have to lecture me,' I cried. 'We're not in school now.'

I turned to go, but he caught my arm. We looked into each other's eyes. He was not angry any longer, only upset, and because I was bewildered, he began to describe an experience to which I had never before heard him refer, nor ever did he after that day.

In 1944 my father was stationed at an airfield in Kent. He and a friend had been granted a weekend's leave, and they took a train to south London. The friend had arranged a rendezvous with his lover, with the intention that all three should go on to a play and to supper in the West End.

It was lunchtime on Saturday, the twenty-fourth of November, as my father and his friend strolled across

61

the road towards the front entrance of Woolworth's in New Cross.

At that moment, something else – something monstrous and inhuman in its conception – approached the rear of the building. Four minutes before, a V2 rocket had risen from a mobile trailer close to the coast of Holland. Sixty miles above the sea, it reached the zenith of a giant parabola, falling back towards the earth, coming down steeply over the quiet Essex countryside, its velocity increasing to three thousand miles per hour. My father pulled open the swing door.

As if opening a door to hell, he saw a dark brown wave flash towards him out of nowhere, blowing him off his feet into the road he had just crossed. Some instinctive impulse made him roll on to his side, draw his knees up to his chin, crook his arm over his head. The world had exploded in one roaring, rushing, deafening sound. He opened his eyes for a split second, and saw through swirling brick dust and flying glass the façade of the building as it began to crumble towards him. Then the rain began – a fierce hail of lumps of masonry and broken bricks which bounced off his curled-up body, fearfully bruising and cutting it. And over all he heard the unforgettably eerie, inverted sound of the V2 rocket arriving, after its reality had already detonated: an explosion followed by the long, dying scream of its engines tailing away into silence.

Then all was night, under a giant cloud of dust and grit, and the moaning and screaming of those close to death, and an age of semi-consciousness and pain ensued, until miraculously my father found that he could free his arms from the debris, to claw his way out from under the rubble. His hands fixed on a large object – something solid, slimy, and covered in stiff hair. The air cleared a little; and with a cry of horror, he discovered in his hands the severed head of a horse.

He turned away, aghast. He could feel no sensation in his legs, hardly knew if they were still trapped, or were freed, only to prove broken and useless. But this consideration suddenly ceased to matter, for alongside him he found his friend, lying up to his neck in a makeshift grave of bricks, shards of glass and concrete, his mouth open, his spectacles shattered and awry. Of the lover who awaited him in the tea room, no trace was ever found.

A hoarse, animal cry welled up in my father's throat, of fear and incomprehension, as wan daylight returned to the scene. Where the building had stood, there was a huge hole in the sky.

My father opened an exercise book and picked up his fountain pen.

'A single building hit by one crudely designed rocket equals one hundred and sixty dead and two hundred injured. *That's* why I give money to CND, Tom.'

'I'm sorry,' I said. 'But why did you never tell me this before?'

'Isn't one supposed to remember pleasure and to forget pain? Besides, when you were small, I got it into my head that a father's role was to protect his offspring from the unpleasant aspects of life. On that score, perhaps, you could accuse me of taking a Victorian attitude.'

He began to mark an essay in the exercise book, reading intently, underlining words with red ink, entering comments in the margin. I remained standing by his side, lost for words.

'But your friend . . .' I began hesitantly. 'If he was standing so close to you, why did you survive whilst he was killed?'

He stared out of the window.

'Oh, there's no mystery, no second thoughts on the part of Atropos. The answer couldn't be simpler. You see, a moment before the rocket landed, I breathed in, and he breathed out.'

Chapter Nine

My father proves to be a suitable second choice for the appointment as a junior history master at the school in Wandsworth. Following this confirmation at his interview, he also receives a recommendation for lodgings. Thus he finds himself, shortly afterwards, to be the temporary inhabitant of a dreary bedsit in Clapham South.

His landlady – Mrs Batsford – takes an unwholesome interest in his affairs from the start. Breakfasts are not only characterized by an unpalatable combination of powdered egg and oleaginous bacon, but also by an intolerable stream of questions concerning his past and his role in the war. Then during the evenings, whilst he is trying to work up his lessons, more than likely he will be interrupted by a knock at his door. Mrs Batsford will enter, upon some transparent pretext, and then will recline, literally for hours upon end, in an armchair, sighing frequently, painting her fingernails with blood-red varnish, chattering interminably about her sailor husband who 'copped it off one of them bleedin' torpedoes' – all the time squirming in her seat and crossing and uncrossing her legs with much rustling of rayon undergarments, immune to hints as to the lateness of the hour, or to the urgency of the work which my father has in hand.

And the days are equally dispiriting, as my father

attempts to transport juvenile minds to the empires of Macedonia and Assyria. To sustain him, he has only the prospect of the long-delayed meeting with the woman he loves.

All through that crucial day a dense brown fog suffocates the city, plunging the midday into premature twilight, leaving the sky devoid of birds and the dismal streets half-deserted. My father paces listlessly around his room, stopping by the window now and then to survey the garden and the landscape beyond, which lie under an unfathomable lake of fog. Outside the world has abandoned all distinctness, as lines and contours dissolve, perspective collapses into obscurity, and colours drain away to sepia.

The dank, insidious smoke of the afternoon penetrates everything, insinuating itself into the house through every crack in the window frames and doors, stealing down the chimneys, crawling into the cellar and squeezing through the floorboards, until it permeates the atmosphere of his room with a grimy mist.

The objects around him break out in a cold sweat and his clothes become damp against his skin. Still he remains by the window, as the room fills up with fumes of boredom and unhappiness.

The garden droops under the weight of this sodden afternoon whilst beyond, at the end of reality, the startled trees, their silvery arms aloft, surrender themselves to the enveloping clouds which shut out the light and mock the dripping sundial standing at the centre of the lawn. Time, confounded and shadowless, seems to pause with uncertainty, as the sunless hours lose track of their divisions and so become mysteriously elongated.

*　　*　　*

The appointed time comes and goes, and my father paces nervously about at the exit from Clapham South station. The fog has thickened with the coming of night and only a few vehicles pass slowly by, their fog-lamps driving yellow tunnels through the vaporous air.

At last she comes, emerging like some beautiful Eurydice from the Underworld of the past. She takes his arm and they set off, walking by the Common, merely exchanging pleasantries at first. But their voices sound unnatural – dry and toneless in the thick air – so they walk on in silence.

There is no sound but for their deadened footfalls in an endless, anonymous street. After a while they seem not to be moving at all, as electric halos glide slowly overhead; and after each street lamp has filed past a black gulf swims towards them, before another swirling and sulphurous light passes on into the unreal night. Occasionally dark silhouettes of bombed-out buildings fade in and out of vision. At last they reach the welcoming lights of a public house.

Over drinks, my father endeavours to be at his most entertaining, relishing the sound of her laughter at his anecdotes of the appalling breakfasts he has suffered each morning at the hands of Mrs Batsford, and of the erotic temptations endured nightly in her company.

All too soon they must go out into the fogbound world. My father, his resolve strengthened by Scotch, takes her hand as they retrace their steps.

'Don't you think that, out of all this, something positive could come?'

'Yes, I do,' she replies. 'Now nobody would be insane enough to start another war.'

His question has missed its mark, but he has been

67

lonely for too long, has buried too much inside, to be anything but inept in the subtleties of courtship. Now his tone takes on a desperate urgency.

'No, I mean in a personal sense. You see, at my father's house, I felt so empty . . . so much in despair, there were times that I truly wished I'd died when the rocket came.'

She stops abruptly under a street lamp and gazes into my father's eyes.

'You must *never* say that again,' she tells him, with a look of horror and compassion. '*Never* think it.'

'I suppose I should be glad to be alive,' he confesses. 'But I'm not . . . or at least I can't be without you.'

She does not reply, but walks on slowly. Although my father has rehearsed whatever it was that he intended to say, the speech is all of a sudden nowhere to be found in his memory, so he launches, unscripted, into a clumsy, amorous plea.

'I shall never again be happy in my life . . . unless you'll marry me.'

'Your unhappiness is nothing to do with me,' she replies gently. 'You had an awful experience. Your best friend died by your side. But things will become clearer and more bearable in time. I've seen it happen to many patients.'

My father turns to her and grasps her hands.

'Listen to me. I'm nothing now. I'm weak with emptiness. But you're strong. One day when I'm strong again, and perhaps you can't bear the world, I'll do for you what you've done for me. I'll do it because I love you more than anything in life.'

The woman smiles.

'You really are an extraordinary man.'

'Only because you've made me so.'

'So I'd be a fool to neglect my handiwork?'

My father nods.

'Then I'd better not be a fool.'

They embrace; my father kisses her cheek. He breathes in the perfume of her neck and hair and closes his eyes. But he cannot prevent himself from weeping. He must weep the tears of purgation, of misery and joyfulness, which burst uncontrollably through his eyelids, must utter the sobs that rise in his throat.

Withdraw. Leave my mother and father alone there for these precious, intimate moments, under a flickering street lamp in a London fog.

Part Two

Chapter Ten

Within a year of these events my grandfather, Elias Crane, died at the age of seventy-six years. He died in an open field, under a billowing summer sky, seated in his folding chair, from which he had been contemplating the blank spaces of his final, unfinished canvas.

My father told me, years later, that he had found it hard to grieve deeply for his father, for he had acknowledged the fact since early manhood that he would never fathom Elias's secretive, guarded nature. The fifty-one years – a twofold generation gap – which separated them formed an unbridgeable space, so that any possibility of intimacy between them was foredoomed. And as my grandfather died almost a decade before my birth, I was denied any living memory of his odd, reclusive lifestyle.

At first my parents planned to keep on the country house as a holiday retreat from London, and spent two summers there. But as they had married and had purchased a house in Richmond, with their increasing financial commitments they found it hard to maintain two properties on a schoolmaster's salary. In the end they decided to sell my grandfather's house.

During a spring vacation my father found himself once again the sole traveller on that lonely country lane which led to the farmhouse, coming this time not on foot but in a newly acquired Austin 7 motorcar, and with the final objective not of renovating the property, but of selling it, and salvaging or disposing of its contents.

For weeks on end he sorted through wardrobes of clothes, shelves of books and drawers full of papers, and searched ruthlessly through tea-chests in the attic and the cellar, where he rediscovered the toys of his childhood. He auctioned these off, together with desperate relics of furniture, and despatched wellington boots, raincoats, hats (he is to be forgiven for not noticing that one of these bore the label of Joseph Mallory & Co.) and hideous ornaments to worthy charities. He committed a mountain of useless bric-a-brac to the flames of innumerable bonfires, for he found that only a tiny proportion of the household contents was worthy of salvation. So that when all this was achieved, and the sale of the property had been finalized, my father was able to convey the entirety of what he had salvaged back to London in the boot of his Austin 7. He drove away with one tea-chest of books, papers and photograph albums, one oil painting and one deed box.

My father had discovered this deed box under a tumulus of stiff and mud-encrusted boots, odorous woollen socks and mould-ridden trousers, in the bottom of a wardrobe in his father's bedroom.

He fetched a bunch of keys which hung on a nail inside the door of the larder, tried all of them and found that none fitted the lock of this box. Anxious not to dispose of anything of interest or value, he took a hammer and chisel to it. The box proved hardier than he expected, and he had virtually to gouge the lock from the surrounding wood before the lid yielded to his efforts.

Inside the deed box my father discovered two things: an old photograph, and a fragment of a letter.

Exhausted by his efforts with the hammer and chisel, he sat down upon his father's bed to inspect these witnesses to past events. He held in his hands a sepia-tinged photograph – a group portrait – finding that it was somewhat overexposed. The inscription on the back of the photograph, executed in a neat rounded script, read: 'The Reverend Mr Southley and Mrs Southley with their daughter and Mr Crane at Holly Lodge, Newlyn.'

The photograph showed an elderly man of stern aspect – an appearance which was compounded by his clergyman's dress – who was seated in a garden chair by a low grassy bank. To his left stood a scowling woman, her hair parted severely in the middle, who was regarding the other two members of this group composition with an expression of suspicion and reproach. On the bank sat a bearded man, apparently in his early twenties. He was attired in a dark suit, light waistcoat, high collar and bow tie. The man was holding a book, and reading to a girl of fifteen or sixteen years. Although the figure of this man lacked definition, as he had evidently moved during the early stages of the exposure and his own blurred and ghostly image exuded from him, this figure was nonetheless unmistakably that of my grandfather.

My father then turned his attention to the letter. The paper on which it was written was well-preserved, and in the script – apparently executed in great haste or agitation, with excisions of phrases – my father could not fail to recognize his father's hand.

The letter was dated 6 May 1889, with the place of composition given only as 'The City of Rome'. It was addressed to 'The Reverend Mr Southley, The Vicarage, Chapel Street, Penzance, England'.

Sir,
By the time this letter reaches you, I have no doubt that you will have learnt the very worst. Although you have every justification to deny me ~~everything~~ all forgiveness, I cannot desist from writing to express my sorrow and penitence at what has come to pass. If only I could reveal to you ~~my misery and suffering~~ one thousandth of the torments I now endure, this fraction would surely convince you of the magnitude of my entire misery and suffering

Here the letter ended, unfinished, unsigned and apparently never sent – or at least never sent in this version.

My father remained seated on the bed for some time, considering these two strange and fragmentary elements of a mystery. But the solution to any riddle can only be inferred from the evidence it contains. And my father had never heard Elias state, or even hint that he had travelled to Rome or Penzance, or had ever known the Reverend Southley and family.

He replaced the photograph and the letter in the deed box. And yet, because these two clues whispered of some long-passed, inexplicable tragedy, they had intrigued my father enough to save them from the flames. The box and its enigmatic contents were thus conveyed to London. All else was left in the hands of the local estate agent, and so the house passed out of my father's ownership into that of an enlightened entrepreneur, who considered respect for the dignity and age of a building to be mere sentimentality. He promptly demolished it to create a handsome estate of pebble-dashed semi-detached houses on the land.

Some years later when my father happened to be in that part of the country, he made a detour in order to see again the place where he had been born, having no inkling of the fate of the house. He drove along the lane, thought his memory had become deranged, turned the car around and went by once more. The unbearable truth could no longer be denied, and with it came an overwhelming sense of powerlessness and remorse. There was nothing left to do but to lay his head upon the steering wheel and weep for the passing of an atom of history.

Over many years, my father forgot – or imagined that he had forgotten – about the existence of the letter and the photograph. But as the memory of his father receded into the past, the puzzle which endured was germinating into an obsession. As Elias had rarely spoken of his life, my father began to think in terms of private rather than public history, especially as his teaching career approached its end.

He 'rediscovered' the evidence, and suddenly began to apply his mind to it with alarming intensity, often reading the letter aloud over the dinner table and speculating as to its possible meanings. Then he would protest over and over again that his father had never once mentioned that he had spent any time in Penzance or Rome. Then he would pore for hours over the photograph, muttering to himself that it was a curious thing.

As these matters engaged him more and more he would try my mother's patience to the limit, so that she would burst out in exasperation.

'For God's sake, you've had that letter and that photograph stuck in a drawer for thirty years! What on earth can you do about them now? The whole thing's becoming absurd.'

My father would frown and blink, as if he had been personally insulted.

'I just don't understand it, that's all. If I could only understand what it all refers to, then I could rest from it.'

'Then why don't you stop talking about it and try to *prove* something? Then perhaps we'll have some peace.'

Unwittingly her words proved fateful, for they were the embarkation point from which my father set off on a long journey which led him deep into his own past and his memories, and beyond, into the unknown land of his ancestry.

And so we are able to redeem the past, and in particular the fate of a small girl, whom we left in the remarkable occupation of sham Siamese twin, in a box of tricks called 'Day's Exhibition of Curiosities'.

Chapter Eleven

The front door slammed, there were racing footsteps on the stairs and my father burst into my bedroom. He was wearing a tweed overcoat and a trilby hat, on the curling brim of which white crystals of snow were still glistening. He brandished a sheaf of pages on to which he had apparently transcribed some lengthy document. His face was ruddy, not so much with the external cold of a winter's evening, but with some uncontainable inner excitement. And his speech was garbled, not so much by breathlessness as by an irrepressible sense of triumph.

'Tom, listen. I tracked him down – the son of Abraham! It's quite incredible. Living in St Ives. You won't believe this – but he actually has *Southley's original diaries*!'

I could not rise to the heights of ecstasy which this revelation had afforded my father.

'That sounds promising,' I ventured uncertainly.

'*Promising*? Why, it's a discovery of inestimable importance. It's the key. Look! Read it for yourself!'

He thrust the bundle of papers into my hands. For a minute or two I scanned the pages with a spurious air of concentration: they dealt with a subject only marginally more stimulating than my homework.

'Well, yes . . . this does look interesting . . .'

'My son is a master of understatement.'

He snatched the pages from my hands as if they represented some sacred and priceless work of art which I was in danger of smashing, or was simply unworthy of handling.

He clutched them to his chest, now talking to himself alone.

'I simply must go through these notes tonight . . . they extend far beyond my highest expectations . . . but I suppose I'd better show them to your mother first.'

'She'll be fascinated,' I rejoined.

But he was gone, holding the papers to his breast like an amulet which could ward off all irony.

Now, fifteen years later, I have my father's transcript of the Reverend Southley's diaries on the desk before me. Over that decade and a half I have changed beyond recognition: what I once despised in my father I have now come to love and admire; and the things which mattered to him then, which seemed to me to be of no significance whatsoever, have risen in my estimation to the point where such memories fill me with shame. So I must set down now what he had discovered.

23rd September 1871

Last night I slept heavily, but my dear wife was awoken in the dead of the night by the crying of cats in the churchyard. Their prolonged, wailing, half-human cries disturbed her, so that she could not fall back into her sleep. So much did the strange sound vex her that in the end she donned her robe and went outside into the night.

It was a warm night out of doors with a fine

rain falling, but no wind, and the sea was calm and whispering in the distance. She took no lamp, but slowly negotiated a course between the gravestones, meaning to send these troublesome creatures upon their way.

She followed the sound until by the graveyard wall – with her eyes now becoming accustomed to the darkness – she espied what she at first took to be a discarded rug. But it was from this unlikely source that the noise seemed to emanate.

There she found a newborn child, wrapped only in this thin and filthy blanket, cruelly abandoned to the elements.

At once she conveyed the miserable bundle into the vicarage and immediately prepared some warm milk for the baby to drink, our housekeeper being not present, of course, at such an hour of the night.

At dawn, she woke me.

'I have found a child,' she whispered to me. 'A child abandoned in the graveyard.'

'What work of the Devil is this?' I retorted, and rose at once to behold the infant.

My wife regarded me with a meek and imploring expression.

'Why must it be the work of the Devil, and not the work of God?' she asked me.

I cannot but recall the hours of that by now dawning day. How I stopped all whom I met in the street with questions. How I knocked on a hundred doors in Penzance without eliciting a single grain of information. How my mood grew black, and my clothes were thoroughly soaked through, for the rain persisted all day. How, as night fell, I ventured to Newlyn.

As darkness rolled in from the sea, my footsteps led me to the harbour. Close to the sheds in which the gutting, cleaning and packing of fish takes place, there is a nest of mean and squalid cottages slumped together in a narrow street, their roofs tilting together, as if they wish to hide the evils they house from the eye of God. In the narrow alleyways of this place the overpowering smell of rotting fish gives to the air an odour of corruption. Here Sin can be glimpsed through every window; it lies in doorways in the form of intoxicated men and women. Yet I was not afeared, for I had come as the wrathful agent of God.

In the pitch dark of that alleyway I could see a faint light shed from a window. Then from within I could hear voices murmuring as if in some unholy incantation, but could make no sense of these garbled utterances.

Without hesitation I knocked loudly with my stick upon the door. I heard movement from within, and then the door opened a fraction. I saw the face of an old woman. She held a lighted candle which threw a macabre light upon her face, ravaged and pitted by the bitter fruits of her sinful life. The flesh of her nose had all but fallen away. Then I knew I had found the place I sought.

'This is the house of the Devil!' I proclaimed.

I pushed my way into the room. The old woman resisted me, but I cast her aside. Within, illuminated by the pale yellow candlelight, such a vision infected my sight as I shall never forget so long as I live.

Upon a filthy bed lay a man and a woman in such a state of indecency, and engaged upon such a foul and unnatural act, I dare not record it. So abandoned were they to their lust, they did not cease from satiating it at my interruption.

In this despicable abode the air assailed me with the disgusting stenches of human excrement, tobacco and liquor, to such an extent that it made my gorge rise. It smelt – I can only describe it thus – it smelt of Death – the Death of all Goodness, Humanity and Virtue. It was the breath of Hell itself.

And then my eyes beheld in succession two appalling sights, so that now I question the reality of what I witnessed, thinking it to be some trickery of the light, or of my reeling senses. Yet, for sure, there lay in the corner of the room *the corpse of a dog*. This was no fresh corpse, but one entirely decaying, so that it pulsated with maggots before my eyes.

I uttered a cry of disgust and stepped backwards to steady myself against a table, only to find that my hand touched a sheet which was drenched in blood – *the blood of a birth!*

Throughout this nightmarish ordeal the old woman was shouting oaths and curses at me in a dialect which I could not understand, nor wished to. I was unable to remain there a second longer and fell, almost in a faint, out of the door. I ran, but I could not go far, for I could not hold down the contents of my stomach.

After this evacuation I leant against the wall in dismay and horror, only to hear, issuing from that abominable place, *the sound of mocking laughter*. That laughter, the laughter of the Devil, will haunt me to my grave.

I write this late at night, with the memories all too vivid in my mind. But after these dark events my task was still not finished. I was determined to discover the truth.

At the end of the alleyway there lay a small inn. I flung open the door with a great crash, and those within fell instantly to silence, knowing by my appearance there that the liquor which they wantonly consumed was dissolving away their souls. I stood as a terrible vision upon the threshold.

'In that house of iniquity,' I declared, pointing down the alleyway, 'a child was born last night, was it not?'

All remained in terrified silence for a while, for they saw my eyes ablaze with the wrath of God.

'Do not trifle with me!' I shouted. 'Was it not so?'

At last the landlord nodded his head.

'Then you had best reveal to me the whereabouts of the mother and father!'

And so I questioned them all without mercy, promising the fires of Hell to those who withheld the truth. And so I came at last to that truth.

*   *   *

It seems that many months ago a travelling circus passed through Newlyn. A young woman who had been attached to that evil enterprise had consorted with a man of the village, so that she remained, when the circus moved away, to dwell with him in that disreputable house in which they had pursued all carnal inclinations. By night they had wasted their lives at the inn, in a state of perpetual intoxication. But she had become with child and the man had deserted her, abandoning her to her fate. She had given birth, the landlord told me, on the previous day, for all had heard her cries. But by the evening she had disappeared. It was thought that she might have gone in search of the man who fathered this illegitimate child. Nothing more was known of her, barring the fact that she was known as Mary.

Thus I went wearily home to find that the child was sleeping, with my wife in attendance. Such disgraceful revelations as I had discovered, I could not naturally make to her. And so I retired at once, alone, to my study, where I found myself weeping and beseeching God to guide me in this sad affair. I had looked upon the child's face. In that face I saw that Innocence dwelt. Thus I consulted my conscience, and it told me that the child must be baptized and so plucked from the very jaws of Hell. It is the only Christian course. I shall take upon myself the responsibilities for the child, which the sins of others have denied her. It is the will of God, and I set this down to shewe how Goodness may spring from Evil.

The Reverend Southley kept his diaries with Victorian assiduity. The nineteen extant volumes, with their beautiful marbled covers, spanning the years 1871 to 1889, which my ecstatic father had found to be in the possession of Southley's grandson testify to this. But it may be necessary to point out that the preceding episode is the single extract from the diaries which could be described as sensational.

One can read innumerable arid entries in these journals which concern nothing more engaging than matters of parish business, or tedious and dogmatic speculations on the doctrines of Primitive Methodism.

It is to my father's credit, I suppose, that he could bear to suffer the mind-numbing experience of absorbing every word penned by the Reverend Southley, in the hope that he would find a diamond buried in a mountain of coal. But he did so, and here is the diamond he discovered.

12th October 1888

By the evening of the 7th the great storm was raging at its most fearsome, and rain was falling at an unprecedented rate. I would say that nearly three inches had fallen in the previous twenty-four hours. All manner of disasters were let loose. A French ship had been driven ashore in Mount's Bay and the lifeboat called to her aid.

Many houses were already flooded, as the sea defences had been breached in several places, and it is a wonder that no life was lost, not least our son's.

We know now that, with no chance of the children returning from Newlyn in such inclement weather, their aunt had sent them safely to bed.

By some means Abraham slipped from the house, fascinated by the wildness of the weather, and came to the bridge of St Peter's church. There he paused, regarding the waters racing below him. However, this structure could not withstand the power of the water and collapsed into the flood.

An inexorable river swept down The Coombe, bearing Abraham with it. I know not how, but he at last gained a hold upon a corner of a building, whilst the seething waters carried all else with them. To be sure, only God's intervention saved him!

For mercifully his cries for help were heard by several people gathered in an upper room of a house. These goodly people threw open the window and peered into the darkness, no doubt incredulous that any human being might have ventured into a night such as that.

A more terrifying vision could hardly have been created in Hell for those witnesses of the raging sky, the dark torrent of the flood, the clamorous thunder and the driving rain. Yet one man climbed from the window, hung for a perilous second, then plunged into the river. His friends must have been aghast at this act, as he disappeared into that awful blackness, and certain that he would be lost.

Nevertheless he struck out against the water's headlong rush, making towards the cries of our son.

I cannot tell how long he was cast about at the flood's mercy, only that, by some miracle, he was not swept away, and at last reached the half-drowned child.

He lifted the boy clear of the water and then, without a moment's faltering, turned back across the river, struggling towards the light of the window.

By God's grace he reached the wall of the house, found a foothold on the lower window-sill, and from there was able to lift the boy into the arms of his friends, and to climb to safety himself.

Now that Abraham has been returned safely here I have punished him for his foolhardiness, and he understands that he placed in jeopardy more than his own life.

As for Mr Crane – for I have learnt that is his name – I have wasted no time in despatching a letter to him conveying my gratitude and inviting him to visit me at his pleasure.

I know little about him, other than that he was not born in these parts but has made Newlyn his home, and is a painter hereabouts.

Chapter Twelve

Swaying along a lane midnight dark, falling dizzily on to its verges, colliding with hedges, pausing to vomit copiously over a five-barred gate, comes my dead-drunk great-grandfather . . .

He comes from the village tavern, from the enacting of his nightly ritual, by which he plays out his role as the local squire. It is always the same: as the evening progresses, his voice and his imagination grow bloated with drink. If you were a stranger in the tavern you might be taken in by the stories he pours forth – of his wounding in the Crimea (he will obligingly roll up his trouser leg to display the long blue-black scar) and his daring in battle. He would tell you how, as a sergeant major, his men loved and feared him; how he is now legendary in the regiment's history.

The local farmers, tradesmen and labourers have listened politely to these tales hundreds of times before; they have run this gauntlet in all its changing forms and with all its increasing embellishments of the truth. Indeed no-one knows what the truth really was, not even my great-grandfather, who has begun to believe in his own inventions. But neither you, the stranger in the tavern, nor those present who have known him for years, would dare to suggest any element of fabrication in his military reminiscences.

For you can see immediately why he became a

sergeant major; once you look into those unblinking clear blue eyes you are pinned, as if with a sword through the heart. There is a trick of the statue-maker's art – to hollow out the marble pupils of the eyes – so that by an optical illusion one sees what is not there. To gaze into my great-grandfather's eyes gives a similarly uncanny sensation.

And there is sufficient evidence of formidable physical power in the muscular bunching of his shoulders, the sudden aggressive tilting forward of the stocky body from the ramrod straightness which is its natural posture, to make a hardened prizefighter consider carefully the likely outcome of a clash with this middle-aged man.

His mouth shoots words like rapid bullets; his whole bearing speaks of power, authority, the ability to control others. As with many men who have experienced the intense feelings of fear generated on the battlefield, and camaraderie in the barrack room, he returned to the outside world to find it a phantom, a world which hardly exists at all.

Now he lies on his back in a field on this warm spring night, keeping his eyes fixed on a single star which splits into two from time to time, then fuses into a single point of light. When the star no longer divides he knows that he is sober enough to complete the journey home.

He goes, singing snatches of a marching song to himself. He lurches through a copse of trees, bouncing from trunk to trunk, knowing no fear of darkness or solitude, plunging headlong through pale serpents of mist.

He opens the door of the farmhouse: it is silent

within but for the ticking of a tall clock, its face adorned with golden suns and silver moons, which he purchased in Paris on his way back from the war.

Upstairs his small son, Elias, is asleep in the attic room. In his waking moments the boy is beginning to understand that he has been born into a family of which Martinet would have been proud; a house which is run on principles virtually as strict as those imposed by his father on the local workhouse, during his term as its master, in the years after he left the army. Now he is a guardian of that workhouse, and a local magistrate. In such a position his temperament is ideally suited to hammering out harsh sentences on those less fortunate than himself: he personifies society's revenge upon itself.

Amongst the faded gentry of the region, whom he despises, but from whom he borrows a specious respectability, my great-grandfather is a feared man. For that reason, he is tolerated in the company of those who perceive with distaste his lack of education and breeding . . .

Once, Elias, in a rare expansive moment, let slip to my father a detail of the curious disciplinary rituals meted out by his father. As a boy he would be summoned into the drawing room, to make answer for some minor lapse in his conduct. This was the 'court martial'.

Then picture the scene as his father, standing in the torrent of sunlight which pours through the window, so that he appears dazzling, clothed in fire like some vengeful angel, drills the boy to stand to attention, to march upon a square of musty carpet, to go through a succession of parade-ground manoeuvres, to be

91

repeated from the beginning if bungled. At the end of all this, the bronze hand is employed.

This pivoting hand is mounted on a base of polished mahogany. Elias must place his hand underneath the bronze hand; and then, in turn, his father places his hand on top of it, to exert the pressure which will make tears spring into his son's eyes, and will leave the imprint of those four inanimate fingers on the back of his living hand. Then comes the formal admonition.

'The bronze hand is the hand of authority, which will crush yours in its vice, if ever you disobey it. Now get out of my sight . . .'

Such experiences cast the pattern of my grandfather's mind. He emerges from the dark night of that childhood with a reclusive nature, a hatred of authority and routine, and a sense of the importance of secrecy and cunning as twin shields against punishment and pain. These defensive mental habits endure like fortresses in his psychical landscape even when, on achieving manhood, the besieging armies retreat forever.

By necessity Elias works hard at his education. He shows a talent for drawing and painting, because it permits the use of imagination and the scope to be creative beyond the humdrum routines of learning Latin and mathematics. Furthermore, it provides an opportunity to excel in a subject of which his father knows nothing.

At the first evidence of this propensity his father is scornful of its merits and its unmanly connotations. His son has proved a disappointment to him: Elias is neither physically strong nor mentally courageous. The father's dreams of an army life for the boy slowly dissolve. As years go by, and drink casts him more and more adrift, he regards the subject less vehemently, since he must resign himself to the fact that his son has failed him.

But as a result of this Elias is able very subtly to appeal to his father's social pretensions, by suggesting that a knowledge of art is the proper domain of a young gentleman. By stealthily mining this seam of snobbery he is able eventually to persuade his father to engage a private tutor.

By finding this single route to his father's favour, he is to gain what he most desires. After his schooldays are over he proposes obliquely that he should undertake a less grand form of the Grand Tour, before committing himself to serious study for the law. He will travel, broaden his horizons, paint, study architecture and cultivate good manners. The idea at length appeals to his father: it provides the consolation that his son at least intends to play the gentleman, whilst getting him out of his sight for six months. And so he agrees to finance six months travel on the Continent.

My father has spent his final day at school. Home he drives, tired and retired, in possession of a rolled-gold pen and a bottle of vintage port . . .

I am visiting my mother. We are seated, each with a glass of Amontillado, in the spotless lounge, where things know their places: the neatly shelved books; the useless but 'decorative' bric-a-brac and ornaments, acquired on impulse in the street markets of this and other European countries; the paintings and prints which I have loathed ever since I came to consciousness in this house; the hissing gas fire, with its shifting

93

flickers of false flame; the potted cacti on the off-white windowsill, beyond which the daylight of a suburban street in Richmond is dying and fading through the coloured glass of leaded window panes. The front door opens and closes quietly.

'How was your last day?' I ask, as my father wanders uncertainly into the room.

'Fine, fine . . . Er, they gave me a pen . . .'

He delves into his trouser pocket and holds up the implement for us to admire. My mother pronounces it to be a very handsome pen.

'Oh, and a bottle of vintage port . . . Perhaps we'll have a glass later . . .'

He frowns and gazes out of the window. Then he murmurs, almost inaudibly, 'Actually, there's something on my mind. I . . . I must do some work . . .'

'Work!' my mother laughs. 'Aren't you supposed to have given work up today?'

'Well . . . you know . . .'

He shrugs his shoulders, then shuffles out of the room, leaving my mother and myself to gaze disconcertedly into each other's eyes.

A little later I go out into the hall. The study door is closed. I knock gently. After a few seconds he automatically responds with the command to enter. I find him sitting in the unlit room, in the dismal half-light of that late December afternoon, contemplating the rolled-gold pen which lies on the desk before him. He is certainly not working; but I cannot see if he is shedding tears.

'Dad . . . Listen, Dad . . . You must accept that it's the old fashion. You give them thirty-five years devotion, and they give you a pen and a bottle of port. That's just the way it works. Everywhere. In every occupation. You mustn't be so disappointed.'

He swiftly turns on me.

'Exactly!' he exclaims. 'So why can't I savour the moment? I've been trapped in that wretched institution for decades! But now I'm free! Free to do my own work! You'll never know how much I've longed for this moment! It's *fantastic*!'

Then he jumps to his feet, bursts into uncontrollable laughter and dances a manic sailor's hornpipe around his study. I subside into a swivel chair by his desk.

'Christ! And I thought you were upset!'

He seizes me by the shoulders.

'Upset? Not likely. Now the *real* work begins. Have I told you about Grez, Barbizon and Pont-Aven?'

'No. Who were they?'

'They!'

He slumps back into his leather armchair, theatrically dashing a clenched fist against his forehead.

'They! Tom, you never cease to disappoint me. They're not people, they're *places*, boy.'

'I'm thirty-two, Father. I'm hardly a boy!'

'Then it's time you grew up and learned something!'

And so, having come to offer consolation, I must suffer a lecture in art history.

'Do you remember the European tour?'

I nod and sigh.

'Where does Elias go?' my father asks.

'To . . . Grez . . . is that what you said?'

'Precisely! And Barbizon. And Pont-Aven. I've proved it. Now let's fetch that port and I'll tell you everything.'

On a morning in September 1874, Jean François Millet

was disturbed whilst at work in his studio in Barbizon by an unearthly bellowing. Venturing outside, his gaze fell upon an appalling sight. A magnificent stag had fled in terror from the forest of Fontainebleau, with savage hounds in pursuit, until exhaustion had overwhelmed it and the animal had finally collapsed in the garden of the house. So the stag lay down to die in Millet's garden; and like some supernatural portent it seemed to the painter to presage another death, for he had been ill too long.

The death of Millet, following that of Rousseau by six years, did nothing to deter the waves of European and American artists from converging on Barbizon. The place had been sanctified by its association with those two eminent artists. The ancient and beautiful forest of Fontainebleau and the open plain to the west continued to be extremely attractive to those eager to cast off the strictures of studio work, with its lifeless classical traditions of redundant mythologies and stylized nudes. Apart from the possibilities for *plein air* painting, Barbizon offered the artist – who, more likely than not, was the victim of an inhibiting Victorian upbringing – the liberating prospect of life in a Bohemian colony. Such a method of working and such a way of life had, ironically, appealed perhaps less to Millet than to any other artist in the Fontainebleau region, since he had rarely worked out of doors and had shunned the frivolous social life of Barbizon.

This social life centred on the Hotel Siron, which stood opposite Millet's house. The dining-room – its walls decorated with silhouettes of the artists in residence, an out-of-tune piano waiting expectantly in a corner – provided the setting for the extended evening meals, the swilling of cider, wine and vermouth, and the desultory discussions on art, which compensated a good many of the participants for their lack of true dedication to hard work. And in the adjacent billiard room too many painters developed a more skilful technique with the cue than they would ever display with the brush.

It is, as my father points out, a question of originality and individuality ironed out by communal living: those who live and work closely together, and sit daily in judgement upon each other's works, will in the end arrive at a consensus aesthetic.

Thus out of this flourishing period of Barbizon's artistic history came few works which transcend the genre: those who painted there are now largely forgotten; one whose individuality might have made him well-known today – Carl Hill – ended his days in a Swedish asylum, his mind plunging into a madness mirrored in crazed drawings, which can only amaze the eye and chill the heart.

And so, with the decline of Barbizon, the artistic focus shifted to nearby Grez-sur-Loire, where many Scandinavian artists had established themselves. This village displayed a melancholy face to the world, with its houses of grey stone and slate roofs, its medieval church and castle ruins.

But Grez could offer what Barbizon could not, in the form of running water: a reed-choked river dense with water-lilies, and a bridge with tall pointed arches, which was to become a favourite motif of the village painters. And in respect of accommodation, the Pension Chevillon provided all the home comforts which a Bohemian artist had come to expect.

Today you can leave Paris on the Autoroute du

Soleil and reach Barbizon in half an hour or so. Now the modern-day water-colourists and potters charge high prices for indifferent works, the legacy of the artists' colony which thrived there a century ago. Drive on to Grez, and the legacy is less apparent. The village has changed little, for tourists do not favour it, and no real attempt is made to market an artistic heritage. Grez, it seems, has lost its memory.

Elias Crane would doubtless have visited both Barbizon and Grez, but his primary destination lay – as it had for the shifting community of painters who discovered a new realm of inspiration a decade before – in Brittany, at Pont-Aven.

By the late 1870s, Brittany had become the most popular region of France for landscape painters. Those who were in flight from their own age, bent on escaping the satanic flowering of the cities and the machine tyranny of industrial growth, imagined that they had found an isolated, unchanged world, bleak and primitive, which was yet a kind of sunless Arcadia, whose inhabitants lived innocent and otiose lives. This vision could never be anything less than fanciful. No doubt the artists were very grateful to take advantage of the modern roads and railways which had penetrated the domain; doubtless they turned a blind eye to the new land-reclamation schemes and the revolutionary improvements in agricultural methods; and they soon found that the rural inhabitants bathed twice in a lifetime, drank heavily and were fond of coarse stories. But, at the very least, they had discovered a haunted landscape, invested with supernatural significances.

Beneath the glowering, overcast skies, windswept

moorlands ran monotonously down to the sea's shifting greyness. Here and there erosion had raised up defiant fists of granite, whilst human hands and Druid minds had dotted the featureless countryside with the standing stones of dolmens and menhirs. There one might come upon Calvaries piled high with human bones, and all the enduring artefacts of the Celtic culture which had been hastily transplanted from England with the coming of the Angles, Saxons and Jutes.

This Breton culture, with its rich folklore and secular traditions so closely interwoven with profound Catholic beliefs, and with its language, orientally rooted and outlawed by the French government, seemed to these nineteenth-century artistic interlopers to symbolize the romantic archetype of a world on the point of extinction. The history of the Breton people, in its resistance to Parisian control, signified a spirit of obstinate independence with which these artists, in their own melancholic resistance to the modern world, could sympathize. In art, my father observes, the 'radical' and the 'reactionary' are frequently keen to jump into the same bed.

And besides, from a pictorial point of view, there was much to recommend the figure in the landscape. The traditional Breton costume lent itself to paint, its various styles determined, in the case of women, by age, status in the community and the possession or otherwise of virginity. Women would wear the *coiffe* in its diverse forms – low, high, narrow or full – made of pure white lace or cotton, to conceal every strand of their hair that would otherwise have tumbled to the small of the back. Their full white collars would be offset by black dresses with voluminous skirts.

By tradition the men appeared in low black wide-brimmed hats, dark jackets cut short, loose woollen waistcoats and wooden shoes.

This archaic society is the setting into which Elias Crane intends to venture in 1887. The plan, instilled in his mind by his well-travelled tutor, has burgeoned in this direction. But he has concealed the precise nature of his journey from his father. It is true that a sojourn in Paris is his first admitted intention; but instead of moving on into Italy to kneel before the nobilities of Renaissance art and architecture in Rome, Venice, Florence, Pisa and Bologna, he will take instead the overnight train from Paris to Quimper. Then two hours in a mail coach drawn by four horses will bring him to the village square of Pont-Aven late the next evening.

Here he will find a small settlement composed of heterogeneous cottages, shops and mills, which has grown up haphazardly beside the rapidly flowing Aven river. And he will find a welcome place to stay in the Pension Gloanec. He will enjoy the motley company of his fellow artists in residence who gather nightly in the red-tiled dining-room, flanked by huge oak tables, the centrepiece of which is a blazing log fireplace over which a gigantic iron pot of soup constantly simmers.

Dinner will be characterized by lavish merriment, and generous portions of plain food and cider. Then coffee will be served out of doors at wooden benches and tables in the village square.

So hereabouts Elias may enjoy some unhurried sketching, for there are innumerable views which provide picturesque subjects. He will make acquaintance with many bearded Bohemian artists. He will learn to flout convention by wearing a straw hat at all times, or stripping to sandals and shorts when the sun appears. But he will not be immune to the occupational hazards of Pont-Aven, in the form of plagues of fleas and large doses of cold inclement weather.

After two or three months he will be lured along the coast to Concarneau, where the dense narrow streets of the medieval town, inhabited by the poor, rub uneasy shoulders with their more affluent neighbours – streets of middle-class houses and artists' studios – a town which presents an altogether different challenge.

Concarneau's sardine industry often impregnates its atmosphere to a repulsive degree. Not long before Elias's arrival there for a stay at the Hotel des Voyageurs, an outbreak of smallpox sent processions of coffins along every street. Yet the faded sails of the fishing fleet, once dyed in dazzling hues, present a breathtaking spectacle as the small boats set out from the harbour at the break of dawn.

The sea also offers itself in all its threatening magnitude to the painters who have created hitherto only the tranquil water-colours yielded by the running rivers of Grez and Pont-Aven.

In Concarneau Elias can witness other extraordinary spectacles. For the American artists organize Fourth of July celebrations, marked by feasting and dancing and fireworks. Their cries of 'Vive L'Amérique' are rejoined by native shouts of 'Vive La France'. And here one might unwittingly stumble upon a fiercely contested game of baseball, staged in a field designed for painting.

My grandfather had learnt of the reputation of an artist,

during his stay at the Pension Gloanec, which has grown to gargantuan status in our day. Yet Gauguin arrived in Pont-Aven as devoid of auguries for a brilliant future as did Elias Crane. For Gauguin was middle-aged, had been a stockbroker for twelve years, and would doubtless have remained so, had he not been dismissed from his post as a result of the crash on the Paris stock exchange in 1882.

Whilst my grandfather is occupying the hotel room which Gauguin left the previous winter, the latter is painting on the island of Martinique. By the time Gauguin returns to Pont-Aven in February 1888, my grandfather has left for England. And so the possibility of Elias sharing a dinner table with this remarkable painter remains an historical lacuna.

The square around which my grandfather strolled during the day, and in which he sat down in the evening to linger over his after-dinner coffee, is now, of course, named the Place Gauguin.

So six months rapidly dissolve, and Elias must return to England, to the family home. He does so with great apprehension, for he has written letters to his father and mother which purport to have been despatched from Rome, Venice, Florence, Pisa and Bologna, describing the wholesome yet totally fictitious artistic endeavours upon which he has been engaged – missives which were, in reality, composed and posted in Barbizon, Grez or Pont-Aven. He has gambled upon his father's general indifference to all things concerning his son, and on his mother's failing eyesight, in his assumption that neither will scrutinize the postmark or the stamp.

Though he returns to the family home in Cheshire

with mounting trepidation, he finds to his surprise that he is welcomed back with unexpected warmth by his parents, and is greeted with news which startles him.

For his father has boasted among the parish officials that his son is a gentleman painter who has been taking instruction from Italian masters, with the result that an unexpected proposition has been forthcoming: that Elias should be commissioned, at a very generous fee, to paint a group portrait of the worthy gentlemen of the town's Masonic Lodge. All concerns for his son's career in the law seem suddenly to have vanished from the father's thoughts.

So Elias wastes no time in setting to work. He gathers together his eminent subjects for preliminary drawings, arranging the composition on the principles of a famous Rembrandt painting. The sitters don their finest clothes and assume their most sombre and smug expressions, to be suitably dignified on canvas. He executes the painting with satisfactory results over a period of four months, and so collects his fee.

But a new plan has taken shape in his mind, in the light of this fortuitous commission. For, before his departure to France, Elias had visited the Royal Academy and had seen exhibited there a painting by the English artist Stanhope Forbes, entitled 'Fish Sale on a Cornish Beach'. Elias later learnt more of Forbes's artistic ideals during his stay in Pont-Aven, and knew that he had become a resident of the Cornish town of Newlyn, where that painting had been created. Elias was now certain of his next destination.

Chapter Thirteen

When my grandfather, Elias Crane, emerges from Penzance railway station in the late, seagull-crying afternoon of a summer's day in 1888, he straightaway finds a carriage in Market Jew Street, to convey his belongings to his new house. He steps into the horse-drawn cab, then instantly changes his mind and dismounts from it, instructing the driver to proceed without him to the address and paying him the fare. Then he makes his way down towards the sea front, to saunter along the promenade.

To his right, the angular skyline of the town's roofs and chimneys is dominated by the high square tower of the church of St Mary the Virgin, beyond which the ochre disc of the sun is beginning to fall; to his left, the fortress of St Michael's Mount is melting into enchanted unreality beneath the turquoise wash of evening. Out in the bay a motionless typhoon of smoke from a steamboat hangs in the air, and a hundred tall-masted fishing boats are stuck like helpless insects to the web of waves in the dead heat of the early evening. Along the shoreline the sea is receding, being pulled back gently over the rim of the horizon. It retreats with a rustling of blue silk. On the looking-glass sands bathing machines are moving to and from the water's edge, drawn by ponies. Men cluster around beached vessels, mending nets and sealing hulls with coal tar, shading their heads from the low sun under Penzance boaters. The shouts of seagulls and fish-jousters fly from the strand where the kelp gatherers are slowly loading the panniérs borne by ancient donkeys, to mingle with the conversations and laughter of the promenaders who stroll or sit through the burnt-out afternoon: the women in long dresses and summer hats, faces shaded under parasols; and the men in dark-suited discomfort. Straight ahead the arm of land that forms the western rim of Mount's Bay, curving hazily in the distance, cradles the shimmering village of Newlyn, its small white buildings stacked haphazardly upon the vertiginous hillside.

Once there, Elias proceeds up the Coombe, past St Peter's church, and stops at last before a large stone-built house which is set back from the lane. A long garden path separates an overgrown croquet lawn from unweeded flower beds. A painted sign on the gate declares this place to be Holly Lodge.

Before he enters by the gate to take in the baggage which the coachman has deposited under the porch, Elias walks a little farther up the lane to survey the house, as it basks in the sunshine and seclusion, from a side aspect. Seeing that there is, as promised, a conservatory at the rear, he nods in approval.

Elias's excitement grows as he unlocks the front door and carries his baggage into the hall. First he explores the downstairs rooms, which he is pleased to discover contain no furniture whatsoever. Each room he enters smells faintly of dampness; but the atmosphere of the house is one of sleeping expectation, as though it has been waiting patiently for the advent of its next tenant.

Elias decides that he will only need to occupy the ground-floor. There is a drawing room at the front of the house; behind this lies another spacious room, by way of which one may enter the conservatory or the adjoining kitchen. This room will become his studio, where he will store his materials and do such indoor work as he is able. So he wanders about, familiarizing himself with the idiosyncrasies of his new habitation – the cracks in the plaster of the walls, the undulations of the flagstones in the kitchen, the rhythmic dripping of a tap, the square of hillside topped by a copse of trees which he can survey from the conservatory. He makes mental notes of the things he will need to furnish him with a modicum of comfort, and concludes that here he will be happy and here he will work hard.

On the following morning he is delighted to chance upon Oppenheim's Great Furnishing Mart, whilst he is taking an investigatory stroll through Penzance town. At once he goes to withdraw some of the money which he has transferred to the local Bolitho bank, which is a sum of several hundred pounds. He spent only a fraction of the money allotted to him by his father for his European tour by living cheaply in France, and has since added to that capital with his commission for the portrait of those eminent Masons. He becomes the possessor of a large sturdy table with four chairs, a stool on which to paint, a dressing-table and a chaise longue on which he will sleep in his studio.

In this way Elias begins to settle into his temporary dwelling, and during the autumn of 1888 he accustoms himself to the pleasures and vicissitudes of his new life. He has solitude, freedom and financial independence; yet on the other hand, the *plein air* painter must contend not only with the climate, but also the local population. The former dispenses gales and driving rain; whilst the latter exhibits fearful reluctance to be portrayed in its natural environment. Customs cannot be disregarded: men and women alike, held firmly in the stranglehold of Primitive Methodism, strongly disapprove of those who paint on Sundays.

To compound the frustration caused to the artist by their unwillingness to act as models, Newlyners often seem only too anxious to form a crowd on the wrong side of the canvas, making concentration on his work a matter of considerable difficulty.

Nevertheless Elias's commitment to his painting is undiminished, and he is constantly buoyed up by his contacts with other artists in the community. Let us examine a typical day of inclement weather – 7th October, for example (which, I should add in order not to deceive you, will culminate in an untypical night) – in the life of Elias Crane.

He rises early and eats breakfast before entering the glasshouse to contemplate the drawing or painting which he has executed on the previous day. Then he walks for a while by the sea, turning over ideas for pictures in his mind.

The old harbour seethes with activity. East coast fishing boats are jammed together by the dockside, landing their huge catches of pilchards. Their masts and elaborate rigging cast stark, shifting patterns against swirling clouds the colour of bruises. There are mountains of pungent barrels and wicker baskets, where the fish are being packed for export to Italy and other Mediterranean countries. Nearby a Scandinavian vessel is unloading massive spars of timber.

On this particular morning a fierce and icy wind is blowing. At the threat of worse weather to come, fishing boats are running for the safety of the harbour. Consequently Elias does not remain long outdoors but calls on an acquaintance in the village, to converse with him for an hour or so and to drink a glass or two of cider. Then he hurriedly returns to his house, as the rain has begun to fall in fitful showers, to start his work in earnest at mid-morning.

As rain drums on the glasshouse roof Elias remains by the stove in his studio, absorbed in sketching out roughly the form of an ambitious painting, until late afternoon when the light dies completely and he becomes conscious suddenly of the outside world and of his need to eat and rest.

As night falls, he decides to take up an invitation to join a gathering of artists at a painter's studio, which occupies a floor above a warehouse not far from Holly Lodge.

As he steps out into the darkness he is astonished by the force of the rain, which hurls itself into his face and penetrates his clothes in seconds. But he dashes through the torrential downpour, arriving breathless and drenched at the studio, where an animated crowd has gathered around a welcome log fire.

He passes an hour or so in talk and drinking whilst the wind and rain rattle at the windows, unheeded by those safe within, and the night fulminates with thunder. But a sudden deafening roar of water cuts short all conversation. The guests crowd around the windows and gaze down, to see – in the incandescent brilliance of a flash of lightning – not a winding muddy street with a stream running by its side, but a foaming torrent of rainwater which is rushing down The Coombe from the bridge of St Peter's church.

The men at the window exchange anxious looks as

the flood continues to rise steadily up the side of the building. Then there comes the rending sound of a tree uprooted and cast against the warehouse by the force of the waters. In the brief silence which this shock induces Elias hears with horror a faint cry from outside, but exclamations of panic from within the room instantly ensue. Elias calls for silence; the noise abates, and everyone is listening, straining to hear through the storm. Then another, unmistakable cry can be heard, and Elias at once throws open the window to an implosion of wind and rain, searching for the source of those cries for help amidst the tumultuous and forbidding river below.

Chapter Fourteen

'But I haven't yet decided precisely where I'm going,' I protest.

My father, sitting opposite me at his kitchen table, gestures dismissively.

'Then if that's the case, what can be the impediment to visiting Grez, Barbizon and Pont-Aven? You'll have a car, so we're merely contemplating minor detours.'

He fits a new needle into a hypodermic syringe.

'Dad, they might prove to be *major* detours. It all depends where I am. After all, it's supposed to be a holiday for me, not a bloody travelling scholarship.'

He peers over his glasses at me.

'Listen, Tom. I've become too geriatric to traipse round France. I'm simply not as fit for all that stuff as I used to be. But,' he adds, carefully forcing the needle through the top of a small phial of colourless liquid, 'you know how much I'd like some detail – photographs, your eyewitness descriptions, notes on the landscape, the hotels they used. It's desperately important to what I'm doing.'

I take a deep breath.

'I know it is . . . I'll see what I can do.'

'Good boy!' he rejoins.

He has drawn up the liquid so that it half-fills the body of the syringe. He holds it up, studying the barrel and pressing gently on the plunger, to eject a tiny arc of glinting silver droplets into the air. Then he lays the instrument upon the table, stands up, unbuckles his belt, unzips his fly, drops his trousers to his knees, sits down again, takes up the syringe and begins to force the needle into the upper side of his right thigh. As he does so, the flesh is depressed into a small white crater. I look away with the mingled feelings of squeamishness and embarrassment which I have never been able to master, although this act has been performed in this kitchen each morning and each evening for as long as I can recall.

'This business gets more and more tiresome,' my father remarks in a matter-of-fact tone. 'You see, Tom, the flesh hardens. It turns to marble. I'm not sure whether that's the fault of the insulin, or of the constant injections, or both. Do you know, quite often these days the needle actually bends. I just can't get the bugger to go in.'

This idea sends a shiver through me, but my father is already on his feet, hoisting up his trousers.

Our family has lived with my father's diabetic condition for many, many years. And so my mother and I have been deluded into supposing it is hardly a disease at all, since the victim has been able to live a normal life and to maintain apparently good health for years at a stretch. The disease has worked patiently and insidiously, knowing it will surely have its day. And recently it has begun to assert itself by tipping the mortal balance against my father. Stronger types and stronger doses of insulin have had to be employed in the war he is waging for life.

The cold sweats, the dizzy spells, the feverish interludes have become more frequent. Now the cubes of sugar and the plain biscuits must never be too far away.

Meanwhile his moods grow darker, his depressions deeper. He is sick of a lifetime's consumption of white fish and boiled potatoes. A craving for habits or experiences abjured long ago can sustain itself for decades. Although my father has steadfastly clung to pipe-smoking as his only remaining oral pleasure, his desire for sweet things has never diminished.

He will recall with the articulate relish of a connoisseur of rare wines a certain sherry trifle he ate in 1952, or a certain chocolate gateau he devoured in his pre-diabetic days.

'So it's agreed,' he tells me. 'You'll do a little detective work in France for your aged parent.'

I smile, and so accede to his request.

'Good! Now let's retire to the study, so I can brief you on exactly what I require.'

Chapter Fifteen

Until this fateful moment in his life, Elias Crane had never thought to challenge his father's opinion – that he was endowed neither with physical strength nor mental courage – and so he would always remember the events of this night with a curious feeling of detachment, as though someone else had taken the role of the protagonist.

After only a second's hesitation Elias climbed on to the windowsill, and was nearly swept off by the force of the tempestuous wind. He clung on desperately, then began to lower himself cautiously from that narrow ledge. He hung there for a moment, before he leapt into the flood.

Elias plunged into several feet of icy swirling water; overcome by the shock of the fall and the powerful currents of the freezing river, he could do little but abandon himself to the force of the water. Some twenty feet downstream he at last gained a handhold on a branch of the fallen tree. Blinded by the driving rain, he could see nothing but the black, looming mass of the building on the far side of The Coombe. A loud rumbling filled the air; he realized that this was the noise of a huge water-wheel and that he was now opposite the Tolcarne mill.

Another cry rose above the roaring machinery, and at that instant a fork of lightning fractured the blackness, momentarily illuminating the giant wheel – which was spinning madly – and, by the side of the mill, a small white oval face, bobbing on the turbulent surface of the flood.

With the water swirling around his chest Elias moved slowly alongside the trunk of the tree, as it lay obliquely across the Coombe. His progress was frustrated by the rushing waters and twice he lost his footing, so that he would have been swept further downstream but for the barrier formed by the fallen tree. During the agony of this slow-motion journey he shouted encouragement to the child, who had managed to cling to the wall of the mill. Now that his eyes had accustomed themselves to the darkness, he could set his gaze on the pale beacon of that face. But when he had barely reached a point halfway across the river the child's face suddenly disappeared.

Elias's limbs had turned to lead. Seeing the head vanish beneath the surface, he found himself transfixed with horror. Then the invisible cords which bound him suddenly snapped and he dived under the water, thrusting himself downstream in the desperate hope that he would follow in the path of the body and perhaps overtake it. He grazed his hands against sharp stones on the bed of the stream, but came into contact with no human form. Choking for air, he began to thrash in all directions, in fearful certainty that the child had been transported out of reach in the whirling currents, when miraculously he seized a tiny cold hand. So great was his surprise that he inhaled a mouthful of water, pushing upwards in blind panic, convulsed with retching, but still tightly grasping the hand. He hauled the child's body out of the water. They were still close to the thundering water-wheel.

The body was limp and lifeless in his arms, and he knew that his efforts had been in vain, for the child could not have survived for that full minute under water.

In this assumption, however, Elias was quite mistaken, for time had become elastic and Abraham Southley had, in reality, been drowning for less than ten seconds. Consequently, when Elias lifted the body over his shoulder and dealt it a massive blow between the shoulder blades, he was astounded to find that he set off a series of violent coughs which culminated in a most exquisite proclamation of rebirth – a prolonged scream.

So Elias began his perilous return across the river, stumbling slowly onwards, with the weight of the wailing and struggling boy unbalancing him. At length he reached the place where he had jumped into the water. Above him at the window a cluster of anxious faces looked down. There was a lower window, and Elias lifted Abraham on to the ledge then scrambled up beside him. From this position he was able to lift the boy into a tangle of arms. After this manoeuvre had been performed successfully Elias, too, was helped in at the window. Once he set foot in the room he promptly collapsed, there being no hands spare to steady him, since all were being joined in rapturous applause.

For the rest of that night the group of painters and the small boy remained in the studio above the Coombe. Elias sat by the fire, wrapped in a blanket, Abraham by his side, similarly clad, with their steaming clothes arrayed to dry nearby. Abraham was spoonfed with hot soup whilst he described excitedly and somewhat incomprehensibly how he had come to be drowning. At length he became quite cheerful, and after the frightening events which had occurred the mood of the marooned artists also improved, as they discovered that there was a thrill of adventure to be relished in all this. One fanciful young man, inspired by his own deluge of alcohol, even expressed the wish that he could transform the studio into an ark in which the artists could survive the flood that drowned the rest of the world, and so could recreate a postdiluvian humanity from a colony of painters.

'But where,' asked Elias, who was now much recovered in spirit, 'would you find the woman necessary to beginning the human race afresh? She would have to be a mermaid.'

'By no means,' replied the inspired young man, warming to his theme. 'I would paint her, and then breathe life into the canvas!'

Sometime before dawn, they realized that the wind had dropped, and that the rain was no longer beating at the window pane. The flood would now die down, they decided, and by morning the world would begin to return to normal – speculations that were a source of unspoken regret to several members of the group.

As the morning light began to seep into the room, and one by one the candles were extinguished, Abraham fell into a sound sleep. The painters gathered once more at the window to survey the Coombe.

Light filtered back to the earth to reveal new chaotic forms. The stricken ash tree lay half-submerged in the waves. But the stream, though still swollen, still bursting its banks and flooding the road, was not now racing away so rapidly, and it was evident that the level of water had fallen considerably against the side of the Tolcarne mill. Its water-wheel was no longer revolving furiously. Upstream they could see that the bridge of St Peter's church lay in ruins. Where normally people walked, a small boat slid quietly downstream and passed directly below the window of the studio. It was propelled by a gaunt old oarsman. A grave-faced man in curate's dress was seated in the stern.

Elias awakened Abraham and announced that it was time for the boy to return home. They went down to the ground floor and opened the door in the flooded stairwell, then waded out into the street. Holding Abraham by the hand, Elias led the way from the Coombe to Chywoone Hill. The sea and the wind had subsided; now only a tangy breeze ruffled the great pools of water on the uneven street. A burst of sunshine above fragmenting clouds promised fairer weather.

Work had already begun to restore order after the storm: men and women, their legs blackened by silt, were busy with buckets and shovels all along the rows of squat white cottages. Flooded rooms could be glimpsed through open doors, strange interior seas littered with the flotsam of household objects. Those at work were watched with intent expressions by the very young and the very old, who were still stranded in upper rooms.

The cottage where Abraham had been staying belonged to his aunt and stood in Old Paul Hill, where – by virtue of its higher ground – less havoc had been wreaked by the flood. Elias duly delivered Abraham into the care of the distraught lady. With a mixture of fury and joy she swept the boy into her arms, shouting that the family had spent half the night searching for him after his sister had awoken to discover his absence. Elias explained briefly what had come to pass, and so took his leave.

As he made his way back to Holly Lodge he was struck suddenly by a terrible revelation. Cursing himself for his lack of foresight, he hurried back to the house to find his belated fears were justified. The glasshouse was built on to the back of the property: from his studio three steps led down into this conservatory; outside it, beyond a walled garden, was a steeply rising hillside.

He gazed in helpless horror at the scene inside the glasshouse where there lay a calm lake of rainwater, two feet or so in depth. He had left half a dozen paintings propped against the walls. The door had blown open in the wind; several large paintings had capsized and were floating, face down, whilst the water lapped gently at the other waterlogged pictures. Alone amongst these drowned paintings a single survivor remained, raised high and dry on its easel in the middle of the dull lake – an island of colour amidst canvas shipwrecks.

Several days later, the Reverend Mr Southley dispatched a note to Elias. Having established the identity of his son's saviour, he felt quite naturally that it was only proper to thank this unknown man for his heroic actions. Beyond this, although he did not reveal so much in his note, the Reverend Mr Southley was keen to confirm that the young man's mettle had been

118

forged as an instrument of God's will. Thus he invited Elias to tea at the vicarage of the church of St Mary the Virgin in Penzance.

On the appointed afternoon Elias made his way to Chapel Street. He was shown into a large, cold, austerely furnished sitting room, where Reverend Southley, his wife, Abraham and his sister, Victoria, were assembled.

Reverend Southley, a white-haired elderly man, who presented a severe aspect in his curate's clothes, was nevertheless profuse in his gratitude towards his guest for rescuing his foolhardy son.

'God blessed us with children late in life,' he explained, 'and I am thankful that His will was not to deprive us of our gift.'

Mrs Southley poured weak tepid tea into Elias's cup.

'Now, I gather that you are an artist of sorts,' Reverend Southley was saying, casting a glance at Abraham.

Elias nodded; the Reverend Mr Southley shook his head.

'I cannot make a pretence that I am well-disposed towards the activity of painting that is not of a purely religious nature. Especially on Sundays . . .'

At this point – quite unexpectedly – he smiled broadly at Elias.

'And yet I do not see that painting and doing God's bidding need always be mutually exclusive. Is that the case?'

Into Elias's mind suddenly sprang the image of his father, standing in a torrent of sunlight which poured through a window so that he appeared dazzling, clothed in fire like some vengeful angel. Secrecy and cunning came to his aid.

'I spend my Sundays in prayer and devotion, and would never dream of picture-making on the Sabbath.'

'I am heartened – though not much surprised – to hear you say so.'

Elias tried to reciprocate with a smile that was entirely counterfeit. A dismal silence fell; a grandfather clock ticked laboriously; every so often came the tintinnabulation of delicate china cups and saucers meeting.

'I know there is a cult of artists hereabouts,' the Reverend Mr Southley continued at length. 'Then tell me what it concerns. I am of an open mind. I was at Cambridge. I take pains in writing sermons. There is an art to this, I would propose, although in my case the matter is all theological.'

Elias then described, in terms which he chose most carefully to avoid any offence, the meaning of *plein air* painting, its origins in Barbizon, Grez and Pont-Aven and the ambitions of its devotees to realize their principles in Newlyn. No naked Arcadian figures strayed into this description; no drunken Bohemian painters lurched into the scene. All was wholesomeness, light, fresh air and the conveying of the unfallen beauty of nature.

To his surprise Elias found that Reverend Southley listened attentively, asked pertinent questions, and eventually seemed almost sympathetic to such a pursuit of painting. He could not decide whether his host's degree of concordance with such a life arose from mere politeness and gratitude, or from that fleeting moment of fascination in which the devout soul can regard the profligate with envious eyes. As if to call Southley back from the brink of temptation, the church bell struck the hour.

'Perhaps there is matter in this for a sermon,' he mused, rising to his feet.

Mrs Southley, Abraham and Victoria, who had remained silent throughout this meeting, also stood, to offer their hands. As he took her hand Elias looked into Victoria's eyes. Throughout his visit she had sat stiffly and sullen-faced on the couch beside her brother, and her gaze had wilfully avoided his own. He regarded the face – pale, small-mouthed, but with dark express-ive eyes – and detected a slight softening of her expression as she said goodbye. She could not have been more than sixteen years old, yet something in her bearing and her poise, the knowingness which haunted her demeanour, suggested a greater maturity.

Before he left Elias invited the Southley family to tea at Holly Lodge, adding that he would be delighted to show them any works in progress.

'There would have been more to display,' he explained, 'but, by my own negligence, several paint-ings were lost on the night of the storm.'

The Reverend Mr Southley showed Elias to the door and placed his hand upon the younger man's shoulder.

'It seems that, in saving my son, you sacrificed your works. Tell me if there is any way by which I might provide some recompense.'

'I expect no compensation,' answered Elias.

'Yet it was a most worthy act.'

'I did only what my instincts told me.'

Reverend Southley patted Elias on the back – awkwardly, for it was a rare demonstration of personal affection – and then, lost in awed contemplation of the ability of ordinary mortals to do good deeds with no thought for themselves, watched Elias go, until he passed out of sight along Chapel Street.

*   *   *

It was on a fine mild afternoon, when the wind blew from the sea in warm moist gusts, that the Southley family visited Elias at Holly Lodge. He came to the gate to meet them smartly dressed in a dark suit, silk waistcoat, high starched collar and bow tie, gave them tea in his sitting room, and then ushered them into the glasshouse to show his work to them.

After the flood he had been left with only a number of drawings and one major work in progress. In this painting depicting a beach scene, there was a vista of flat sand dotted with figures, which melted into a calm sea that mirrored the metallic greys of an overcast sky. In the foreground the viewer looked down upon a small fishing boat, by the stern of which the figure of a fisherman was taking shape, as was that of a boy kneeling on the sand. A coil of rope lay before him, snaking into his hands. The boy was looking up questioningly; the fisherman was bending towards him, pointing to the rope. Evidently he was teaching the boy how to tie a complex knot.

The Reverend Mr Southley nodded and frowned, divining nothing remarkable in the scene, so that he could think of no apt comment. At a loss, he therefore simply enquired as to the title of the work.

'I think I shall call this "Golden Rules",' announced Elias. 'The old fisherman, you see, is demonstrating one of the fundamental rules of seamanship, in the making of good knots.'

'Indeed, indeed, I see that . . .' Reverend Southley responded, still unable to detect any significant meaning in the work, but musing over the possibility that the inspiration for the painting might have a biblical origin.

'The technique is square brush,' Elias continued.

'And is this . . . near completion?'

'By no means,' Elias laughed. 'First I must work another figure into this group in the foreground, though I must say it is hard to come by models. Then it will take some considerable time to perfect the composition, to bring out the natural quality of all that is depicted.'

Later Elias carried chairs on to the lawn, so that they might sit in the weak afternoon sunshine. In the garden the conversation continued rather falteringly between the two men. But above all, this second encounter with the Southley family confirmed Elias's suspicion that the wife and the children lived in silent fear of its head. Then a sudden inspiration gave him the opportunity to confound their exclusion.

'I have recently acquired a camera,' he informed the Reverend Mr Southley. 'It is not of the most modern kind, but I have had good results with it and I find, also, that it can help me in my painting. I wonder if you would permit me to take a photograph of you and your family?'

'May not such a box of tricks appeal most subtly to the sitter's vanity?'

'Some say worse of it. Certain primitive peoples believe it can steal away your very soul, but no Christian man or woman in England today would give credence to such superstition. The camera merely holds up a mirror to nature – where it sees vanity it will record it. Think of it in this way – the camera will preserve a moment in time, which can never be repeated. It will recall our good fellowship and this beautiful afternoon. And who would dispute that both these blessings are God-given things?'

123

'Indeed, I am mindful of your words,' Reverend Southley deliberated, 'and in the light of them, I believe I can offer no serious objection to your proposal.'

As he went indoors to fetch the camera, Elias smiled smugly to himself: how a little cunning blended with hypocrisy will tie any killjoy curate in knots!

He set up the tripod and camera on the lawn, then gave instructions as to how the subjects should be posed for compositional effect. He positioned Reverend Southley's chair by a low grassy bank. His wife was to stand beside him.

'Let's have Abraham and Victoria together, seated on the bank,' he suggested from behind the camera.

Abraham at once scrambled into place, whilst Victoria reluctantly followed, her sullen expression unchanged in spite of the novelty of the situation.

Elias licked his fingers and raised his arm above his head.

'The wind is in the east,' he announced. 'Consequently, I shall increase the exposure time by one second.'

All was ready.

'Wait a moment,' interjected the Reverend Mr Southley. 'Would it not be more fitting if you were to appear in the photograph, as you are our host?'

'I should like that very much,' Elias replied, 'but then, of course, there would be no-one to operate the camera.'

'I'll do it!' exclaimed Abraham.

'Surely a child is incapable of doing so,' declared Reverend Southley.

'Yet it is simply a matter of opening and closing the shutter for the correct exposure time,' Elias rejoined.

'Then by all means let Abraham perform this.'

The boy joined Elias behind the camera. After a minute or so, he appeared to understand what actions were required of him.

Elias took up a position beside Victoria, whose gaze was, as ever, averted from his. Then he suddenly stood up again.

'I feel it would lend a naturalness to the composition if it appeared that I were reading to Miss Southley.'

Before Reverend Southley had the opportunity to insist that the text should be of an acceptably wholesome nature, Elias hurried into the house, then returned with the first volume which had come to hand.

'Now we are ready,' he proclaimed.

Abraham began the exposure – somewhat prematurely in his excitement – before Elias had settled in his place and had taken up his pose, with the open book upon his lap. During this time, he drew a stern and lingering look from Mrs Southley.

The boy succeeded, however, in closing the shutter promptly, after the collodion plate had been exposed for the period computed by Elias.

Chapter Sixteen

As Elias returned to Holly Lodge after a morning's stroll some days later, he was passed in the lane by a procession of weather-beaten caravans. Eight horse-drawn wagons, all of which had once enjoyed colourful coats of paint, went by him in their noisy progress down to the village of Newlyn.

He broke off from his work in the middle of the afternoon to saunter down the Coombe in search of this travelling fair, which had established itself on some open ground beyond the road and the stream, close by the Tolcarne mill. It had occurred to him that this spectacle – with its cast of itinerant characters, its lively sideshows and attractions – represented an ancient annual ritual in the region, one which might easily yield itself to his artistic purposes.

A large crowd, consisting mainly of the mothers and children of the village, had already assembled, swarming amidst the merry-go-rounds, swings, Aunt Sallies and sideshows, where the air was filled with the enticing odours of hot gingerbread, apples and roast chestnuts.

Elias wandered here and there in the throng, musing on how he might best approach this subject in paint, when he caught sight of a familiar face.

Victoria Southley had stopped before a sideshow. It

was named DAY'S EXHIBITION OF CURIOSITIES. She was gazing intently at the painted scenes on the panels of the wooden hall. On an impulse, Elias went quietly to her side.

'Grotesque, are they not, Miss Southley?' he said suddenly.

Victoria spun round, her expression full of alarm. Elias smiled at her and raised his hat. But once she had recognized him she offered no greeting, only an icy stare from below the brim of her bonnet.

'They are all absurd fakes,' she hissed, casting a glance over his shoulder in the direction of a local photographer named John Gibson, who was preparing to take a photograph of the crowd in front of the Exhibition of Curiosities.

Incidentally, it is thanks once more to my father's diligent research that, in writing this, I have the advantage of referring to a reproduction of that very exposure in an obscure book of early photographs of Penzance and Newlyn. But that, you may say with justification, is quite beside the point; what matters is what happens next. Then let me detain you no longer . . .

Victoria turned away at once from Elias and went as hastily as she could through the crowd. He set off in pursuit, and caught up with her as she hurried away from the fairground.

They left a few moments before a figure – more bent, more bronchitic, more mildewed and more mottled with the passage of time – mounted the platform to deliver his oration. For over three decades – since last we met him – Matthew Day continued to play the part

127

of showman and mountebank. With him, his 'curiosities' aged; the years ensured that his tiny moving village became ramshackled, that the transportable scenery faded like a long-forgotten dream. For after many thousands of miles of journeying, he simply failed to make his fortune. And within a year Matthew Day was to die in his sleep, in that strange pungent caravan, watched over by an audience of grinning and weeping masks.

'You appear to have no time to spare,' Elias suggested, as he caught up with Victoria.

'No, you are mistaken,' she answered, staring straight ahead. 'I simply did not wish to be photographed there. Nevertheless, I am expected to return home directly I have visited my aunt.'

'Yet I can see little harm in enjoying the spectacle of a travelling fair.'

'My father considers that fairs are a source of sin, because fair people do not worship at church. He says that they conduct their lives outside the laws of God.'

'Perhaps so,' Elias ventured. 'Then so must I, since I am never to be found in a church. If he knew as much, I dare say he would consider me no better than these gypsies.'

They had reached the lower bridge across the stream. Victoria stopped and leaned against the parapet, looking upstream towards the fair.

'You are quite wrong,' she replied disdainfully. 'My father has a great respect for you, because you saved that idiot boy from drowning.'

Elias also leaned against the parapet, half-turning towards her, but offering no reply. At length she began to blush under the provocation of his scrutiny and shot a glance at him.

'Do not expect *me* to be impressed by what you did.'

Elias reacted with a shrug.

'I never asked you to praise me for it.'

Then after a pause, in which his irritation mounted, he added, 'I fear you have been reading too many novels. To be so haughty, like a heroine.'

'You are mistaken again,' she replied coolly. 'Father forbids them. They also are a source of sin, you understand.'

Without another word she turned to leave, abandoning Elias on the bridge. After a few seconds, he decided to follow her.

'May I accompany you for a while?' he asked when he was once more by her side.

'It is of no consequence to me whether you do so or not,' she answered, setting a brisk pace.

They continued in silence, until they had left the outskirts of Newlyn and were following the promenade towards the faint lights of Penzance. The sea was high and a fine mist was sweeping inland; in the gathering dusk they moved away from the brilliant beacon of the Lighthouse Pier, beyond which a fishing fleet had set sail on the evening tide. They were now alone on the broad promenade. Victoria slowed her pace, as though some failure of resolution had finally drained her of mobility.

She went to the edge of the sea and grasped the iron rail, looking down into the scurrying waves below.

'Forgive me,' she said quietly. 'I spoke . . . spitefully to you. I should have thanked you for saving Abraham.'

Elias muttered words to the effect that he was not offended. They stared out to sea for several minutes, until the horizon had been obliterated by a phantom tide of approaching fog banks.

'Come, let's continue,' he said gently.

As they went on, wordlessly, Elias became acutely conscious of the characteristics which made his companion increasingly intriguing to him. He had never before been exposed to such a potent mixture of insouciance and vulnerability. It took the form of a tantalizing mystery in his mind, for he perceived that some great strength of will coupled with some great sadness had conspired within Victoria to make her the person she was. Locked in such a background, he wondered how such characteristics could have arisen: this experience within youth, this worldliness born out of innocence. Then he thought of his own past, and realized such things should never be sources of surprise to an outsider. He decided to trespass into that perilous region.

'You live very much in the shadow of your father's beliefs, don't you?'

Her tone became contemptuous once more.

'I am not impressed by them,' she answered curtly.

He laughed. 'Those are surely dangerous words for the child of a curate-in-charge.'

She flashed a defiant look at him, which made him consider whether she objected merely to the substance of the challenge, or rather to his reference to her as a child. As if to demonstrate her independence of mind, she announced that she had admired Elias's painting.

'Only because your father did not,' he replied in a teasing tone.

'Perhaps,' she murmured. 'All the same, I should like you to paint me.'

Elias was profoundly shocked.

'To paint *you*? But your father would never

approve,' he told her incredulously. 'How could you imagine such a thing?'

'How dull you are! Why must my father know of it?'

As she laughed, Elias was suddenly afforded a fleeting glimpse of vivacity unmasked. He took a deep breath.

'It's true that I do need another figure – of a girl – for the painting which I showed to you. Unfortunately, I fear it would not prove suitable for you, since she should be the daughter of a fishwife.'

'Then I shall dress as one,' Victoria insisted. 'I can find a dozen old dresses at home. Mother and Father distribute them to the poor of the parish.'

'But if your father should discover us!' Elias exclaimed.

'How could he? I am allowed frequent visits to my aunt in Newlyn. If we are discreet, he need never suspect.'

Elias thrust his hands into his coat pockets.

'This is pure whimsy,' he told her. 'I have come here to paint the reality of things. What, in truth, can you – a clergyman's daughter – know of the world of fisher people?'

'I can imagine such a thing,' she protested.

'No, you cannot. And so perhaps you had better see it for yourself. Let us return to Newlyn.'

Victoria raised no objection and they went back in silence to the town. As they reached the granite arm of the new North Pier and passed by the ice-making works, Elias led the way up a steep and narrow street.

Late October was bringing to an end the season for pilchard fishing, but a large catch had just been landed at the harbour. As darkness fell, men, women, children and donkeys were hauling baskets and barrels of fish in torchlit processions up from the slipway. Sometimes two or three people would manhandle a barrel between them; or old women would labour up the slope with a basket of fish supported by a cowal – a band across the head, by which the burden was transported.

In the dark street the smell of fish became overpowering; Elias heard Victoria retch.

'Would you rather go homewards?' he asked her.

'No,' she replied, with as much bravado as she could muster. 'I am eager to see whatever you wish to show me.'

They continued, and as they ascended the street the cobblestones grew wet and sticky beneath their feet.

'The street is so muddy,' Victoria remarked.

'It is not muddy,' Elias replied. 'It is running with blood.'

Victoria froze in her tracks, but Elias took her by the arm, propelling her onwards.

'Too late to turn back now,' he murmured, relishing her fear and disgust.

Suddenly he ducked through a low doorway, a little wider than the barrels it was made to admit. They emerged into a large stone-paved courtyard, the centre of which lay open to the moon-glazed sky. All around, candles and paraffin lamps made of this infernal scene a moving chiaroscuro, as dozens of figures went about their business, passing in and out of the deep shadows. Elias drew Victoria aside into a block of darkness, where they stood drawing shallow, nauseating breaths from the unbearable atmosphere.

The ancient rituals and processes which Elias and Victoria now observe, together with the place in which the scene is enacted, seem as if they must always have existed; and those living shades who inhabit this putrid nocturnal world never pause to question whether their way of life will go on for ever. They believe that it will, and that the sea which yields them millions of fish each year will never cease to be bounteous in its gifts. Perhaps this blindness is a blessing, for the reality is that their world is slowly coming to an end: the sea will give and give until it can give no more. And so this way of life is to disappear, leaving not a vestige for our age.

But now there is much work to be done. Around the sides of the courtyard are ranged cellars, where cured fish are in storage. The upper storey of the buildings comprises the living quarters of the industrious denizens, who must sleep in the rising stench of their livelihood.

The pilchards must be bulked by piling them in alternating layers of fish and salt on the paving stones. In this state they remain for three weeks until they are considered cured. Then they will be washed in huge wooden trays called kieves, to dispense with the scales, before the fish are packed into hogsheads, in circles, head to cask. Then they will be pressed for two or three hours. More fish will be added and pressed, until the hogshead contains some two thousand fish.

All is restless activity, but for a group of women and girls who sit together on upturned barrels, their faces cadaverous in the dim light.

'Now, my little fish girl,' whispered Elias in the darkness, 'you would work here all night long for three-pence an hour. And you would receive a magnificent dinner of bread and cheese, and a small glass of brandy every six hours. Would you find that agree-able?'

'It is horrible,' Victoria gasped, holding a scented handkerchief to her nose.

'It is the life which some people must live,' Elias responded. 'It is a hard life, and a rather ironical one, since the greater part of what these worthy Methodists produce is shipped to Italy. The fishermen have a toast: "Long life to the Pope, Death to our best friends, And may our streets run in blood!" Their best friends are the pilchards, whose blood we have waded through tonight. But now I sense you have seen enough of the new life you proposed to adopt.'

He ushered her through the narrow door. They set off down the hill towards the sea, grateful for gusts of sweeter air, and made for Penzance.

'Now,' Elias laughed, 'after having witnessed that pretty scene, do you still wish to portray the daughter of a fishwife?'

She thought for a few moments.

'It was horrible, and yet it fascinated me. So my answer is yes.'

They progressed in silence towards the lights of the town. Elias felt deeply perturbed by the manner in which this air of conspiracy had enveloped them, so rapidly and unexpectedly, during such an ephemeral encounter. But by the time they had reached the edge of the town, they had chosen a day on which Victoria was to visit Holly Lodge.

After they had said goodbye Victoria hurried into the gathering darkness, leaving Elias alone on the promenade, beset in equal measures by excitement and trepidation, as he dwelt upon the impropriety of this unexpected turn of events.

Chapter Seventeen

Victoria stood transfixed in the glasshouse; she had donned a simple ragged dress, purloined from a chest at the vicarage, a white apron and a black hat; and she was staring intently at a cross which had been chalked on the stone floor of the conservatory. They worked together in silence, but for the sound of Elias's sketching and the occasional bluster of drizzle hurled against the fragile walls. Despite the heat from a small stove, the glasshouse was draughty and cold.

Elias had by now embarked upon a number of preliminary drawings for the figure of the girl which he intended to work into his painting of a beach scene. On each of the occasions when Victoria had come to model for him she had hurriedly changed behind a screen, and then had posed for a half-hour or so, in order that she could reach her aunt's house without arousing suspicion that she had been lingering elsewhere.

During these encounters few words were spoken; and once the available time had expired, Victoria would leave hastily. She remained, however, extremely enthusiastic to continue her work for him, and was always apologetic if she had been called upon to apply herself to other errands, and so had been unable to keep their appointments. Elias found himself looking forward most eagerly to her visits, and if ever she was detained elsewhere he could not concentrate on other tasks. Then he would spend a vacant hour or so gazing from the front window of Holly Lodge down the narrow lane, in the hope that he would catch sight of the small figure, in cloak and hat, marching purposefully uphill towards his house.

Elias put his drawing aside, then drew a silver watch from his waistcoat pocket.

'It is nearly three o'clock. And surely time for you to make your way homewards.'

Her reaction to this remark – a sudden shout of exasperation, followed by a flood of tears – startled him.

'If there were any other place to go,' she cried, 'I would go anywhere but home!'

'But that is foolish talk.'

'Why?' Accompanied by a stamp of the foot.

Elias shrugged his shoulders.

'Because home is where you live, after all.'

Not understanding her torment, he made a feeble gesture to take her in his arms, but instantly she broke away ferociously. Then she appeared to compose herself, drawing deep breaths and drying her eyes with the backs of her hands. He watched her, standing still against the moving backdrop of racing clouds.

'You speak of home,' she murmured, shaking her head violently. 'On my sixteenth birthday, my father summoned me into his presence. I sat before him like some humble, destitute parishioner, in dreadful awe of him, as I always have been. Then he began to explain something which I could hardly begin to understand, the words like those of a foreign language to my ears.

'He told me that he was my spiritual father, and bade

136

me understand that he had sinfully deceived me, and in doing so had performed the Devil's work. He could, he said, no longer withhold what he had to impart to me, since God demands ultimately absolute truth and honesty.

'I was confounded . . . I could only reply that his meaning entirely eluded me, and that, for my part, I had never been untruthful or deceitful.'

Victoria turned suddenly to Elias, her expression hardening to bitterness.

'I can see that man's hands clasping tightly, whilst he spoke to me, as if he wished to crush my soul between his palms.'

She suddenly threw open her arms in a gesture of dismissal.

'Of course, I knew that he had never truly loved me. It was all too evident from the coldness he bore me. But I had never until that moment understood why that was the case.'

Victoria turned away once more, to stare at the landscape beyond the glasshouse, and her voice fell to a whisper.

'He repeated to me that he would always be my spiritual father, but the fact of the matter was that he was not my father in blood.'

Victoria cast a fleeting, sideways glance at Elias.

'Oh yes, and then for good measure he added that my mother was not my mother in blood.'

Now tears began to stream down her face whilst she continued, her speech convulsed with sobs.

'So I protested . . . that it could not be true! That I had always lived with them . . . as my parents . . . that I had loved them as such . . . never imagining . . .'

'And that was not the end . . . he told me that my

mother – then straightaway corrected himself to say "my wife" – was disturbed one night in her sleep. She thought that cats were crying in the graveyard and meant to scare them off. But the cries were mine. I had been abandoned in the graveyard. He said that it had been their Christian duty to take me in . . . to feed me, to grant me life . . . And, in respect of that, I should be eternally grateful to them.'

Victoria turned to stare intently into Elias's eyes.

'You imagine that I broke down then, don't you? That I wept uncontrollably and tore my hair out. I did nothing of the sort. I may have afforded you a glimpse of the misery it caused me, but I was damned if I'd show it to him . . . So I simply asked about the whereabouts of my real father and mother. In reply he lowered his head, fell silent, and began to write his journal for the day.'

Chapter Eighteen

It is late at night. From travelling in my grandfather's
footsteps, I take the Calais to Dover ferry and drive to
London, reaching home in a weary state, to step over
the threshold into a bad dream. I have been driving
around Brittany, going where I pleased day by day, so
that the note which lies on my doormat is the first
intimation that something is wrong. Its four words
speak volumes of dread: '*Ring me urgently, Mum.*'

He is in hospital; a stroke suffered two nights before.
But he is recovering; no permanent damage antici-
pated . . .

I wait anxiously with my mother in a hospital corridor
until the official visiting time begins. At last we are
admitted to his ward. My father is sitting up in bed. He
has a drip-feed into his left wrist, and a monitor for his
heart. It may be fanciful, but I think the heartbeat trace
on the screen above his bed graphically registers his
excitement at my arrival.

We embrace, and I am lost for words. He senses my
dismay, for the close proximity of death brings out the
child in all of us.

'Don't worry,' he tells me, 'I am not yet ready to go to
that unknown country!'

I give him presents; a nineteenth-century landscape

in watercolours, which I picked up in Grez; an out-of-print book on the artists' colony in Brittany, which I came across in an antiquarian bookshop in Concarneau.

'Now I'm bursting to know about your trip,' he says.

'What about telling me about your illness first?'

'Oh, nothing to tell, really. In the study – bad pain in the chest. Worsening. Mum called for the ambulance. Lots of fuss. Much better now, though. Bit groggy, but blame that on the medication. Week inside. That's it. Now, describe the places to me. Are the hotels much the same, do you think?'

My mother and I exchange glances of mock despair. And so I begin to recount my travelling experiences, playing Marco Polo to the Kublai Khan enthroned in his hospital bed.

Indeed, I tell him everything I can remember, sparing no details, throughout the daily visits I make to his bedside.

'This is excellent material,' he says repeatedly. 'Admirable research. You see, I must picture these things in my mind, or I simply can't make connections.'

'You should write it all down, Dad. Keeping notes isn't enough.'

He taps his forehead.

'No. However, it's all stored away up here.'

'But nobody else has the slightest grasp of it.'

'You do, Tom. *You* write it down. You're the writer, for God's sake.'

I shake my head.

'No, I've other fish to fry.'

Yet as I leave, passing along an endless white hospital corridor, I see what is inevitable: that I must write it down. After years of resistance, I am at last enmeshed in the mystery. It torments my thoughts, because I cannot extricate myself from the riddle; and because it is a vital part of my father which will outlive him.

But what kind of story will it be? Not a simple family history. It must be a more exotic stew of fact and imagination. It will be 'old-fashioned' – but after all, I reflect, many of us exist, inwardly if not outwardly, at a vast remove from our modern world.

I reach home and sit down at my desk, a blank sheet of paper before me, my chin cupped in my hand. I make a few desultory notes of ideas; at length, these scribblings begin to elongate themselves into tentative sentences. Although it is very late, and I am tired, I roll a sheet of paper into the typewriter, and begin:

'Past midnight in the darkened house, its silence resounding with the ticking of clocks, and my father still hard at work . . .'

Chapter Nineteen

To prolong their series of meetings Elias executed four preliminary drawings of Victoria, making a pretence that he could not perfect her part in the grouping of the old fisherman, the boy and the girl who watched them. However, with the approach of Christmas, he discovered that he was to be denied her company until the New Year as the family planned to spend two weeks with relatives in Kent, although the Reverend Mr Southley would, of course, return to officiate at all the necessary services.

Elias passed New Year's day alone at Holly Lodge, in a mood of discontentment which veered towards anxiety, although he hardly understood its causes. He sat in the glasshouse, studying every line of the drawings he had made of Victoria, frustrated that he could not transform those lifeless strokes into her living substance. Then he moved across to the screen which concealed her when she changed. The dress she wore to model for him was draped over it. Closing his eyes and trembling, he clutched the coarse fabric against his cheek. It carried a scent – not a manufactured perfume – but some faint, lingering fragrance of her essence. He cast the dress aside, shaking his head violently, as though to shuffle off temptation.

But on the following morning he awoke to find that he had not shed this acute sense of his separation from her. And it remained as torturous for the three days which followed.

On the fourth morning Elias rose in a fever of restlessness. He dressed hurriedly and made his way to Penzance, hoping to quell his unruly emotions by ambling amongst the crowds in Market Jew Street. For most of the morning Elias wandered disconsolately here and there, pausing to peer indifferently into the shop windows of Fleming's the Cabinet Makers, or Oppenheim's Great Furnishing Mart; to draw money from the Bolitho bank; and to observe the coming and going of carriages and carts, conveying such a variety of people and things to and from places, with such a multiplicity of purposes, with such an accompaniment of shouting and interminable bargaining, with so much boarding and alighting of bodies, so much loading and unloading of baggage, so much feeding, cajoling and chastisement of horses and donkeys, that this bewildering complex of activity struck him as unbearably pointless.

He fled, to take lunch at Chadleigh's Eating House, with its distinctive bowed windows and its enticing aroma of chops. Yet the boisterous atmosphere within, the gorging and the swilling, the laughter and the high tide of voices drowned him in oppressiveness.

It was then, as he sat picking at his food, that a dreadful explanation occurred to him: somehow Reverend Southley had discovered that Victoria had been visiting him secretly, and so had forbidden any further meetings.

His throat was dry with nausea; he could swallow no more. He pushed his plate aside, paid his bill and left

Chadleigh's, crossing the road to reach the corner of Chapel Street.

There Elias stood, trembling and sweating, with a pounding heart. It was certain that he must act swiftly; yet he could not help but prevaricate. Drawn by the vertical displays of colourful cards and stationery in the windows of Shaw's Bazaar, he went inside, but in such a trance that it came as a shock to him, when much later he returned to Holly Lodge, to find a paper bag full of envelopes and writing paper in his pocket.

Then he lingered, unseeing, before the elaborate façade of the Egyptian House – that architectural anomaly which still stops tourists in their tracks as they turn into Chapel Street. For his thoughts gravitated elsewhere, drawing his eyes down the street towards the tower of the church of St Mary the Virgin. At last he knew he could hesitate no longer.

The Southley family had just finished lunch. A maid showed Elias into the chilly sitting room, where – shaking in anticipation of an ugly scene – he awaited Southley's entrance, fully expecting to encounter the Reverend's wrath for enticing Victoria into an immoral occupation. Suddenly, after summoning all his courage, he felt incapable of mustering a single argument in his own defence; his whole being seemed to have dissolved into powerless despair. Without warning the Reverend Mr Southley swept majestically into the room, to greet his visitor most warmly and enthusiastically.

The two men took tea together, and passed an hour or so in innocuous conversation. There was no mention of Victoria, and no sign of her during that time. Once Elias thought he heard her voice carry from some remote corner of the house. But by the time he rose to leave she had not revealed herself.

When Elias was almost out of sight of the vicarage he took a final backward glance at the house. He imagined he caught sight of her face, for a fleeting moment, at an upper window. He could not be sure if she had waved briefly before she drew away, nor if this ambiguous gesture signified a helpless imprisonment, or a resolve to flee to him.

But at last Victoria did return to him. He saw her, from his vantage point at the front window of Holly Lodge, striding determinedly up the lane. He ran to meet her halfway down the garden path, grasping her hands fiercely out of anger and relief, whilst tears sprang uncontrollably to his eyes. He raved at her, then demanded, then begged for some explanation of her absence. But she calmly responded that there had been many commitments at home and tactfully withdrew her hands from his, adding the suggestion that there was work to be done, and that time was of the essence.

So she resumed her visits. Elias was working in earnest on the canvas. But he encountered further difficulties, for he could not paint her if the light was unmatched with that of the grey day he had created in 'Golden Rules'. As there was no possibility of painting Victoria in other outdoor scenes, for fear of their being seen, he was forced to wait for days of suitable light. There was no sting in this, however, since she visited him all the same, sitting beside him quietly as he worked at sketches, murmuring comments of approval or disapproval, in so natural a fashion that he soon came to rely upon her as an arbiter of what was right or wrong in his work.

*　　*　　*

On one occasion, as Elias was mixing colours, Victoria picked up a photograph from the table in the workroom. She took up a pen to write an inscription on the back: 'The Reverend Mr Southley, his wife and daughter, with Mr Crane at Holly Lodge.'

'There,' she said. 'You should always write on the back of a photograph. Otherwise, when you are old and your memory is bad, you may not remember the people depicted.'

Her admonitory tone made him burst out with laughter.

'But I am hardly likely to forget *you*!' he responded.

Now I think back to the incalculable hours which my father spent in archives, poring over abstruse wills, convoluted testaments, and a thousand dusty documents in search of the minor details which time had jigsawed into thousands of random pieces in a puzzle, I can begin to understand how it was that he missed the thing which was literally staring him in the face.

Once I had decided that I should write all this down, I took up a semi-permanent residence in my father's temporarily abandoned study whilst he lay in his hospital bed. I had time enough to study the papers and notes, which simply overwhelmed me with the minutiae of things, so that I found myself staring vacantly at the cork notice board. There was the photograph of the Reverend Southley with his wife and daughter, encapsulating the blurred image of my grandfather, Elias Crane. Perhaps I sat there for half an hour or an hour, or two hours, until I realized that the face of the girl was familiar to me – had, in reality, been familiar to me all my life. But how?

Because it existed elsewhere, independently in my memories. That it could only exist in the most obvious place of all will be clear to you, though it was by no means clear to me, nor had it been to my father.

There is a game one can play with the aid of an atlas of the world. You simply select a page – of a country or a continent – silently pick out the name of a village, town, city, or county, then challenge your opponent to guess it, imparting only the first letter as a clue. Psychology dictates that your inexperienced opponent will scour the map for the tiniest village set in minute print, so that you will defeat this opponent if you choose that which is most obvious – the spaced-out lettering for a country, a state, a province, a canton, or a mountain range.

I unpinned the photograph from the notice board, then went into the lounge to compare it with the painting which has hung above the fireplace in this house throughout my life. Of course, the face of Victoria had always been there, its gaze fixed for as long as the painting existed, on the hands of the small boy who was attempting to tie a complicated knot. My father, too, had lived with this painting for most of his life, had even set about cleaning it – only to be severely chastised by his father – at the ancient farmhouse, during those melancholy months after the end of the war.

Too much familiarity with the painting and the photograph had denied my father the revelation. Yet all this was understandable, for in some historical identity parade in which one was searching for the dour-faced daughter of a clergyman, dressed in black, with her dark hair gathered up behind and severely parted in front, one would hardly pick out the ragged

147

daughter of a fisherman, whose tousled hair tumbled down her back. And although the frame of the painting bore a title, 'Golden Rules', the canvas was unsigned, so that my father had never considered the possibility that it could be the single extant painting executed by Elias Crane.

When I had related all this, we sat in silence: I watching the earnest expression on his face; he gazing in an unfocused way out of the hospital window opposite him, which provided the edifying view of a midair corridor connecting his part of the hospital to another identical part.

Suddenly, he shook his head.

'No. It's not the same face.'

'It *is*, Dad.'

A long pause.

'All right. What if it is? Where does that get us to?'

'It turns the key.'

'To what?' He looked me steadfastly in the eye.

'To the letter, of course.'

Victoria lifted her head and broke out of the pose. Elias saw that she had begun to cry.

'I *hate* my father,' she whispered fiercely.

Elias immediately went to her side and took hold of her arm, attempting to soothe her with words. But she drew away, opened the glass door of the conservatory and stepped outside into a sudden brilliant burst of sunshine, as though she had divined its coming by some dramatic magic. Elias followed her.

'Very well, if you can't pose, let's walk for a while,' he suggested.

They went out by the garden gate and slowly ascended the hillside, making towards a small secluded copse. Victoria rubbed her eyes and sniffed; Elias watched beaded tears roll down her cheeks and fall to the grass.

'You cannot hate him,' he told her gently; but she merely shook her head, as if she could find no words to express her confusion.

They walked on in silence.

'In any case,' he added, attempting to lighten her mood, 'dressed as you are at present, you're not a clergyman's daughter at all, but a fisherman's.'

'If I were, I might have a father who loved me,' she answered swiftly. 'One who might love my mother, Abraham and me like a proper father.'

Elias sighed. 'But he has no choice. He must love God before all others.'

'And that makes it right for him to be so cold and tyrannical?' she asked tremulously.

Elias could not respond, so deeply was he disturbed. As they came to the edge of the trees he was overcome with the exhilarating flash of a premonition: that in this moment, as they stood still, a bird sang, a church bell chimed far away, their world was poised in pre-figurement of another.

He touched her arm lightly; she looked into his eyes. Then she broke away from him, with an utterance – half-joyful, half-sobbing – and began slowly to descend the hill. He watched her go, dark head bowed and hands thrust into the pockets of her dress. But he was transfixed by an equipoise of sensations, of triumph and failure, ecstatic yet unbearable.

Something must happen to change the course of this story irrevocably. To witness these events you must take a seat – before the copse of trees above Elias

149

Crane's house – in the place where my father and I once sat down together a century later.

From this vantage point you have a perfect view of the conservatory at the rear of Holly Lodge.

Now follows a spectacle enacted in this glasshouse to make your heart race. A bearded man enters with a dark-haired girl. He sits on a stool by which an easel stands at an angle. The girl appears to be laughing, and twirls round upon her toes, her arms outstretched. The man's mouth is moving – words and then laughter. The girl stands still, then places one foot on the man's knee and begins to unlace her boot. She repeats the actions for the other foot. Then she begins to disrobe.

First she discards her long black dress, unbuttoning it from the neck, slipping the garment from her shoulders, before stepping out of it. There is a moment's hesitation. Some words pass between the couple. You see the man nod his head. The girl unpins her hair. It cascades in a surprisingly long and lustrous fall over her shoulder blades to her waist. She rapidly removes and casts aside her remaining garments, and is suddenly naked.

The man watches intently, but does not move. You are too far away to divine his expression; but by her actions you can be certain that the girl is quite unabashed. She twirls around again, so that the man may study her body through a tantalizing revolution. You suddenly ask yourself: is the scene you are witnessing simply an objective display of eroticism, or a pure expression of naked innocence? Is this designed to incite lust in the man who watches, or to signify the verdant spirit of the unclothed girl?

For a few moments these questions hang in the balance, as you contemplate the slender whiteness of her form, with its small breasts and buttocks, which would seem almost ghostly and insubstantial were it not for the darkness of her nipples and the small black delta of her pubic hair.

The scene freezes, with the girl standing before the painter. He takes up a palette; the brush dances between pools of colour, as he swivels towards the canvas and begins to paint. You cannot see the marks he is creating. Several minutes go by; neither of the figures speaks; then abruptly the painter puts aside his palette and brush, and enfolds the girl in his arms.

She remains transfixed whilst he strokes her hair and kisses her forehead. He is talking to her, his lips close to her ear. Then he takes her by the hand and leads her through the dark doorway, into the house, and out of your sight.

Chapter Twenty

Victoria was seated on the chaise lounge in the workroom of Holly Lodge, her form silhouetted against the lambent noonday light which irradiated the glasshouse beyond her on that spring day in 1889. Elias stood before her, eyes wide in bewilderment, white-faced.

'It is not possible,' he murmured, shaking his head and swallowing with difficulty. 'I have always ... withdrawn from you at the crucial moment . . .'

His voice trailed away.

Victoria reached forward, taking his hand and drawing him towards her. She pressed his hand against her belly but he wrenched himself free, as though he had been invited to caress a barrel of gunpowder.

'I do not think I can be mistaken,' she whispered.

He drew a deep breath, then turned away from her in wild-eyed panic, to pace up and down the studio in a figure of eight around two easels, shaking his head and muttering to himself in helpless incantations, 'God please, no . . . Please God, no . . .'

Suddenly he halted.

'You are quite certain?' he asked forcefully.

'It can be nothing else,' she replied with equal firmness.

Elias stared into the garden. Presently Victoria rose

and went to his side, laying her hand on his arm; he glanced at her and was shocked to find, all of a sudden, that she was smiling.

'I am glad,' she announced defiantly.

'Glad!' exclaimed Elias in horror. 'And what of your father? Will *he* be glad?'

She shrugged her shoulders.

'That is not of importance. What matters now is that we are in love, and must spend the rest of our days together. Of course, we shall run away. To London, I think.'

Elias stared at her incredulously.

'Yes, of course we must run away,' she continued in an unflustered tone. 'Otherwise Father will prevent us from seeing each other ever again. But nobody will know us in London, and so we shall start our new life there.'

He continued to stare at her in disbelief. It was not simply the earth-tremor of this revelation which had destroyed the foundations of his life at a stroke; it was her calmness and indifference to it, her apprehension of their ruin as a trifling difficulty, which cast down all the pillars of reason, logic and common sense.

'To London?' he shouted. 'Don't you think they will find us, wherever we go? And heap shame upon us?'

She lowered her eyes. 'It is not shameful to be in love and to have a child.'

Elias groaned and sat down on the chaise lounge, covering his face with his hands.

'I must think about what is best,' he said, each word heavy with resignation. 'I suppose we have a little time?'

'Oh yes,' Victoria replied cheerfully, 'our child will not show for some time yet.'

During the days that followed Elias spent many hours wandering aimlessly along the coastline, or pacing in his figure of eight around the two easels in his studio. A dozen times he resolved to go directly to Reverend Southley, to confess everything and so fall from the height of his good opinion; then to beg forgiveness and to pledge that he would make amends with a marriage.

But each time his nerve failed him, for he could not bear the visions of Southley's wrath which haunted his waking hours. Morever, he could not truly swear to himself that he loved Victoria. He reflected that, should he make the noble gesture, marriage and fatherhood would dispossess him of the freedom he had grown to cherish. And yet how could he abandon her to face alone the anger and humiliation which certainly awaited her?

From the moment his thoughts had become knotted with so much anguish and so many contradictory impulses, he had felt incapable of applying a single brush stroke to a canvas; and yet his ambitions to become a renowned painter still hovered over all this turmoil.

Thus he would walk with a thousand thoughts wheeling and swooping like birds of prey in his mind. He tried to tell his soul to be calm; he appealed to his intellect to evaluate every contingency in the minutest detail. As he sat contemplating the horizon it was the sound of waves bursting on the rocks below, shattering before their roaring retreat, which instilled at last some tranquillity into his heart.

After all, he reasoned, did not artists frequently make mistresses of their models? Did they not frequently beget children out of wedlock? Yet, he reflected ruefully, such indiscretions were deemed infinitely less shocking to social convention in London or Paris; and whatever their location, such models were hardly likely to be the daughters of clergymen. No clinging to Bohemian mores could assuage the gravity of his own situation, for it would be wholly different for him if he were to flee with Victoria to London. They would be hunted; they would be forced to live in hiding, and therefore in ignominious circumstances, since they would be penniless.

Then he thought of making a confession to his father, wondering if he would assume, as in the past, the role of vengeful angel once he learnt of his son's misdemeanours. But now it was not the bronze hand of his childhood memories which was to be feared as an instrument of physical torture; this had been transformed into an instrument yet more dreadfully powerful, for it was now the human hand which signed the banker's drafts. Without these, his life as an artist would come to an abrupt close.

Elias knew that there existed certain establishments in the reeking, twisting lanes close to Newlyn docks, where his current difficulties might be brought to an end. This same knowledge, of course, lay locked away in the Reverend Mr Southley's heart, as a terrible secret. In a world where impossibilities could be realized, Southley would be able to confirm his young friend's suspicions from first-hand experience – that such establishments are fearful and revolting places, and that no amount of desperation would justify an attempt to entice Victoria into such a hellish remedy for her condition.

By these tortuous paths, Elias realized that no

calmness of soul, no application of intellect could shake one unassailable truth: that his glorious future was dissolving before his eyes. This truth seemed tangible enough to him; but it will not bear our more objective scrutiny, because Elias was ensnared by delusions of his own making. For he not only over-estimated the importance of the position which the Newlyn *plein air* movement would come to occupy in the history of English painting; but, most importantly, he elevated his own mediocre talents far above their worth.

Caught in a net of irrational beliefs and impulses, he convinced himself that this bright, mythical future might still be reclaimed if only they were to escape to France, to live anonymously and cheaply in Brittany or Fontainebleau. Where he would be able to develop his art for four or five years before returning to England, by which time any search for them would surely have been abandoned. But still the same insoluble problems beset him – could he be happy to share with Victoria a life condemned to poverty and obscurity?

For several days, however, this plot seemed to Elias to offer the best solution to his dilemma – a workable compromise by which he would accept his paternal responsibilities, whilst still clinging steadfastly to his artistic aspirations. In the Breton countryside they would not be found; there he was familiar with the customs and the language; there he could count on several acquaintances to aid him, if his circumstances became desperate.

At the same time as he began to lay elaborate plans for this venture he was still fearful that, in the end, he would be scandalously unmasked; that he was prepar-ing only the mere postponement of the ruination of his career to some distant day of reckoning; and thereafter he could see only lifelong disgrace. Disgrace . . . the word dogged him day and night. It lay at the end of every pathway: disgrace, should he flee alone; disgrace, should he flee with Victoria; disgrace, should they confess all now. In every plot he hatched, there lay the fatal flaw of disgrace.

Victoria visited him every few days, and seemed to grow ever more sanguine with thoughts of their new life together. She still favoured an elopement to London although he patiently described the advantages of a life in rural France, to which she began to warm. Some ten days after her revelation Elias had formulated the final plans for escape. Then he told her that he was ready to begin the necessary preparations for their flight, although he warned her that these would take two weeks at least to bring to fruition. In the meantime, he proposed, it would be in their best interests not to meet, lest their plans should be confounded at the last minute. Elias would send word to her when everything was ready.

After she had departed, swearing eternal love and devotion to him, Elias left Holly Lodge and crossed the narrow causeway which led from Street-an-Nowan to Newlyn Town. He wandered amidst the labyrinthine streets, scarcely noticing that, with the coming of spring, the village had taken on its most beautiful aspect; that along every cobbled street and in the maze of narrow alleys and courtyards the cottages were dazzling in their new coats of whitewash, against which burned the vivid, glowing colours of geraniums, fuchsias and flowering vines; and that, in the distance, the town orchestra was playing, the glinting brass instruments raised in tribute to the beaten gold of the young sun.

When he tired of Newlyn he set off for Penzance, wandering the length of the promenade until he came to the harbour. Passing by the harbour office, he found himself standing before the Dolphin tavern, where, a century later, my father was to treat me to an illegal glass of beer for patiently humouring his indulgences.

Five stone steps topped by an iron railing lead Elias to the door of the public house – steep-roofed, in stone painted white, with three sets of chimneys aloft and a mixture of bowed, casement and balcony windows fronting it. Above the door a notice declares a Mr Tyzack as the gentleman licensed to purvey wines, spirits and ales. That is sufficient for Elias: as a man who has worked up a thirst almost tantamount to his despair, he is ready to drink deep.

A plain wooden interior, benches and tables, pipe smoke and the odours of strong drink. Columns of fragile blue sunshine penetrate the dirty windows, to settle crazily on the sawdust-strewn floor. Desultory conversations, aimed mainly at the disparagement of the fishing skills of their near neighbours in Newlyn, die and fall amongst ancient men. They take little notice of the young man who sits alone at a corner table, although we must take a more acute interest in him, for he is about to make the most momentous decision of his life . . .

We notice he is fatigued and self-absorbed: he takes no heed of his surroundings; his face is set; his fingers slowly revolve the glass upon the wet table, his eyes never shifting from contemplation of its contents; occasionally he drags the fingers of his left hand through his hair; then he drains the glass at a single draught, and at once goes purposefully to the bar to have it replenished.

We can watch this sequence of events spin through several revolutions, until a perceptible change occurs. The young man loses interest in his glass: he ceases to turn it upon the table. He leans back; his eyes are focused now not in the near, but the middle distance. Whereas he was frowning not so long ago, the lines on his brow have now slowly melted away. It is as if he has rediscovered the significance of a memory, and as its importance overwhelms him his face becomes suddenly animated, his eyelids flutter rapidly, he straightens up from the drooping posture, broadening his shoulders. As if some abstruse scientific discovery has coalesced in his mind he rises from his seat, leaving his drink unfinished, and rushes into the street.

Elias descended the five stone steps from the tavern and abruptly turned the corner into Quay Street, at the summit of which rose the tower of the church of St Mary the Virgin. There on the wall of the Dolphin he found the poster which had caught his eye for a fleeting second, as he had approached the public house. This poster showed a three-masted steam and sailing ship, and advertised passages to New York. By the time he had finished reading the details his mind was made up. He saw in that instant that he was able to formulate a foolproof plan which he would be perfectly equipped to execute, since he had grown up to wield secrecy and cunning as the twin shields of punishment and pain.

Elias then hurried into the harbour office, in order to make certain preliminary enquiries. Afterwards he walked rapidly homewards, his mind seething with inventions and fabrications. Once he had reached Holly Lodge, he sat down to write four remarkably contradictory letters. I must convey the substances of those letters, bewildering though they may at first appear. But remember: the stratagem behind them was Elias Crane's, not mine . . .

The first letter – addressed to a solicitor in Manchester – informed the recipient that Elias Crane intended to take up permanent residence in Newlyn and made a request for all his available capital and all assets capable of being realized to be transferred at once to the Bolitho bank.

The second letter – to the property agent – stated that Elias intended to return to Manchester in a fortnight's time, and so wished to terminate his agreement for the renting of Holly Lodge.

The third letter was to Victoria, to tell her that it was necessary for him to travel to Manchester for business reasons, and that when he returned to Newlyn – in two weeks or so – they would immediately take flight.

The fourth letter was to his father. This contained the astonishing news of an offer which Elias had received from a wealthy American. This mysterious millionaire, who was both an art dealer and a philanthropist, had been so overwhelmed by Elias's talents that there was now an opportunity for him to begin a new life in America. Once there, he would be ensured of patronage and guaranteed great success under his benefactor's guidance. Now he simply needed sufficient funds to book a passage and to establish himself in New York. He asked his father for as large a sum of money as could reasonably be spared to be transferred to the Bolitho bank.

There remained a fifth letter to write. But at that moment, Elias had no stomach for it . . .

On the following morning he posted three of the four letters in Penzance, then spent a considerable length of time at the Bolitho bank. Afterwards he walked down Chapel Street, which bustled with shoppers and holidaymakers, to purchase a jug of cider at the Turk's Head tavern, standing out in the street as he sipped from his glass.

From this vantage point he was afforded a clear view of the street where it ran past the entrance to the vicarage. He waited anxiously for an hour, praying that Victoria would emerge alone. Then he would greet her as though they were merely acquaintances, and when the opportunity arose, surreptitiously pass the note to her.

But it was Abraham who came out of the vicarage and turned to walk up the street. He was alone, so Elias left the tavern to intercept him. The letter was passed to the boy with instructions that he should convey it to his sister, but on no account to make any mention of the fact to his parents.

'Why?' Abraham enquired.

'Because I intend to give your father a gift . . .' Elias improvised. 'Of a religious painting. This letter is a request to your sister to write to me, to tell me which are his favourite biblical scenes. Then I will paint one and present it to him. But this must remain a secret absolutely, known only to me, you and Miss Southley. Then it will be a complete surprise to your father. Do you understand?'

Abraham nodded enthusiastically, feeling thrilled by this secret arrangement. After ensuring that the letter was safely in the boy's pocket Elias returned to Newlyn, for he had still more preparations to make.

In the shifting community of painters in Newlyn Elias knew that his disappearance would not be interpreted as unusual, or worthy of any suspicion. As most of the artists with whom he had come into contact had remained mere acquaintances, all he had to do was let it be known that he had decided to forsake Newlyn and return to Manchester. Such an eventuality would generate no gossip for the time being. And if ever the scandal were to break, it would make no difference, for he would be far away by then.

That evening, he happens upon a group of painters drinking in a tavern near the Newlyn docks and during the course of their conversation mentions that he must soon depart for Manchester. His case is hardly significant, since most of his colleagues live by the whims of fortune and the lures of more promising places to live and work, and his announcement is quickly forgotten.

The next morning he rises with the dawn, for he needs to purchase a great quantity of food and candles. The food must sustain him for almost two weeks, and there must be a considerable amount of tallow to hand, since he intends to sleep by day and to read or sketch by candlelight after night has fallen, with the shutters of his house tightly closed at all times.

A week passes by; he begins to run short of food, but has lost all interest in eating; he loses track of time; he sleeps fitfully; often he hears a voice talking to him, only to realize with a shock that it is his own. One morning a letter arrives from the property agent, acknowledging the fact that he has terminated his lease. But there has been no letter from his father to confirm the forwarding of money. In the solitude of his nocturnal life he analyses his plans a thousand times, testing them for any fallibilities. His hopes begin to dwindle as time drags itself laboriously by, until – all of a sudden – he is thrown into frenzied activity.

He has no idea what day it is, but as he rises as dusk is falling, there are two letters on the doormat. The first, from his father, confirms in a congratulatory tone that Elias's request for funding has been granted, with a handsome sum now being in transference to the Bolitho bank. The second letter – which has been delivered by Victoria herself, in anticipation of Elias's return from Manchester – seals their fate in three words: 'It is certain.'

There was no time to lose; Elias urgently needed to make several important calls in Penzance. He roused himself to action, for now that his plan had come to fruition one important detail required attention. Thus he took a bowl of water, some soap and a cut-throat razor, and shaved off his beard.

Whilst this change of appearance was being accomplished the weather considerately agreed to conspire with his plans, by providing a torrential downpour to ensure that nobody without a very pressing reason would be the least inclined to venture out of doors.

Elias took an umbrella and – head down, collar up, hat brim pulled down low – dashed through the rain to Penzance. He called first at the Bolitho bank, learning with great relief that all the money he was able to realize had found its way to his account. All of this money he withdrew straightaway. Next he went quickly to Oppenheim's Great Furnishing Mart, where he imparted several strict and explicit instructions to an old retainer who could boast not a single hair on his pate, yet flourished a veritable shrub of coarse grey whiskers on both cheeks. Finally, he hurried to the Harbour Office to complete the arrangements.

Ten days had elapsed since he had first set eyes on the poster on the wall of the Dolphin tavern.

Darkness thins at first light, as a carriage draws up outside Holly Lodge. A bright dawn breaks as the driver loads up the carefully packaged crates which hold a few volumes of verse and prose, sketchbooks, paints and brushes, and the finished canvas, entitled 'Golden Rules', wrapped in sacking and destined to be stored at Oppenheim's Great Furnishing Mart. The occupant of the carriage has left his table and chairs, his chaise longue to the next unknown resident. He has carried with him as personal luggage only a suitcase of clothes and private effects, and a deed box containing papers and photographs.

The first brittle radiance of that May morning carries the promise of a fine day ahead, as the carriage starts for its destination.

Chapter Twenty-One

Now it has happened again, and so I must walk along that endless white hospital corridor, though my legs will hardly carry me, and my heart is icy . . .

My father lies unconscious, imprisoned in a diabetic coma; he may, or may not, have suffered a stroke. I stand by the bedside, contemplating his still face upon the pillow. It is impossible – the force of life which he contains cannot be extinguished; he cannot cease to exist, without some fundamental prop of reality should break forever. It is impossible . . .

Later we sit in the darkened lounge, my mother and I, with our glasses of sherry, our false cheerfulness which barely conceals the mounting hysteria, and soon subsides into silence.

Then suddenly my mother bursts out in a huge tearful sob.

'It's the end,' she cries.

I go down on my knees before her chair, and take her in my arms.

'No it's not . . .' I whisper.

'He may not be right in his mind,' she gasps, unable to catch her breath.

'Of course he will,' I reply, although I have ceased to believe as much.

And then, with the dreadful tolling of doom, the

telephone begins to ring. Startled, we stare into each other's eyes. We are frozen; my mother tries to raise herself, but I gently hold her down in her chair, then go myself to answer the call.

I can hardly speak, can hardly hold the receiver, can hardly believe what I hear. For he has returned from that void, that lacuna in consciousness where nothing exists, the abyss which lies somewhere between life and death, so deep that dreams cannot descend to it. I replace the receiver.

'There. What did I tell you . . .' I say to her nonchalantly, as she stands white-faced at the other end of the hall. 'Father's regained consciousness. I knew he would all along.'

Chapter Twenty-Two

The open carriage swept along the road from Newlyn towards Penzance town. Its passenger, a young man wrapped in a heavy dark cloak, gazed blankly before him, as though he wished to bear away no final remembrances of this dawn, with its strand of mercurial light stretched along the horizon of Mount's Bay.

Blinkered by the certainty that he would never again return to this place, he tried to shut out all impressions, all sights which might transform what had become the familiar and ordinary scenery of his life into something unique, beautiful, irredeemable. To his left the angular skyline of the town appeared, dominated by the high square tower of the church of St Mary the Virgin; to his right, the fortress of St Michael's Mount, standing out to sea as a vast solitary monolith of shadow, now that all other darkness had been eroded by the coming of morning. Such visions Elias Crane refused to see.

The carriage drew up before the railway station. He dismounted from it, still in his cold oblivion. Carrying his personal belongings, he slowly entered the station. Along the wet platform great ice-encrusted boxes of fish – their dead eyes flashing accusing glances – went by on rattling carts, to be hurled with shouts and crashes into the goods wagons. Bulging sacks of letters and parcels stood here and there in unruly mountains, whilst drivers, stokers, engineers, guards, ticket

167

collectors, passengers and porters of the Great Western Railway jostled past him. At the far end of the platform the engine hissed, its firebox casting a dark red glow through the black smoke and pale steam which turned the air damp and grimy, as though the day, hardly begun, had hurried to its twilight.

At the centre of this tumult Elias stood, his thoughts lost in a swirling fog, and waited.

Chapter Twenty-Three

To say that a person has disappeared off the face of the earth is to pander to an absurd cliché, unless – of course – that individual has been buried, or cremated. Yet my grandfather was not dead, buried or burnt . . .

And yet he has disappeared off the face of the world I have made for him. He has, more accurately, slipped away, venturing beyond the bounds of my imagination – at least for the time being. Frankly, I have no idea whatsoever where in the world he may have gone, and I tell my father as much. But first I read aloud to him my account of Elias's fraught departure from Penzance railway station.

My father lies in his hospital bed, gazing out of the window. I sense that the story I am relating to him either displeases or distresses him, although his expression betrays no remarkable transformations. It is by way of his silence that he conveys some disapproval. From time to time I waver from my account, fearing his criticism, afraid of my own literary inadequacy, and so now and then I say: 'Shall I go on?'

'Of course,' he answers, with deadly evenness. 'I'm listening.'

I complete my reading of the chapter, and shuffle the manuscript.

'Well?' I ask at length.

'Do you really think that this . . . version of events . . . approximates to the truth?' he asks.

I shrug my shoulders. Then, with sudden conviction, I reply: 'Yes, I do. Or at the very least I'd say that it fits the facts quite plausibly.'

'The horror of it all,' he pronounces after a few seconds, 'is that it does. And you know what that means, don't you?'

I am not sure that I do; my eyes droop towards the words on the page. He answers his own question with unexpected vehemence.

'It means, Tom, that my father was a moral and mental coward!'

'Perhaps,' I reply. 'But maybe we shouldn't be so hasty to judge, before we can ascertain how all this was resolved.'

My father turns over in the hard bed, his head sinking into the white pillow, as though some invisible weight of fury is impressing it there.

'Where has my blasted father gone?' he whispers fiercely, and this burst of exasperation makes me laugh.

I lay my hand on his shoulder.

'I don't know, Dad. That's what I'm trying to figure out for you . . .'

'Then come back soon . . . and read more to me . . .' he murmurs.

'I won't read to you, if you find it so irksome.'

He grunts.

'History should be as truthful as possible,' he tells me. 'Now make sure you come back soon . . .'

He closes his eyes and yawns. With the quick ebb and flow of his vitality, I see that he is ready to surrender himself to sleep.

'Of course I'll come back,' I reply. 'And so will Elias, by the way.'

But by now I have passed beyond my father's hearing.

Chapter Twenty-Four

On the following morning Elias was roused from sleep by a furious cannonade of rain, as it was hurled in rattling gusts against the flimsy window of his cheap hotel room. He had been dreaming of an underwater world through which he moved in slow motion, where familiar people, set like corroded statues, swam by; and then a smiling child had fixed its lips to his and drawn all the breath from within him, so that he was drowning.

He woke with a start, consulted his pocket watch, and realized with a surge of panic that he had precious little time to spare. He dressed hastily and began to hurry down narrow alleyways, edged by silent and cramped terraces of forlorn houses. Soon he plunged down into winding, cobbled streets, dwarfed on either side by black, towering warehouses. Then alleyways running with rainwater disclosed at various turns dismal expanses of river-grey.

By the time he had reached the docks his clothes were thoroughly saturated, and he rushed through the milling, disgruntled crowds until – through the half-light of the day which refused to break – he perceived a configuration of lines: of masts, rigging, funnels, superstructure, bow and stern, by which he recognized the steam and sailing ship which had been portrayed in the advertisement posted on the wall of the Dolphin tavern.

Here was berthed *The City of Rome*. Yet how can I convey the shock suffered by Elias of its discovery in the world? From an artist's small sketch on a billboard far away had flowered an impulsive idea, which in turn had allowed Elias's fanciful notions of escape to be polarized from their actuality. But now that apparently simple solution to a human dilemma had to be measured against the great broad bulk of its reality.

Here lay *The City of Rome*, no longer a ghost ship, a phantom of the imagination, but an 8,400-ton vessel which had been built originally for the Inman Line and was now sailing under the flag of the Anchor Line; a ship which was replete with seventy-five first-class cabins, two hundred and fifty second-class cabins and one thousand places in steerage; a ship which boasted – if one could afford the price – interior elegance and electric light, and which could convey both the richest and the humblest ticket-holder to New York in seven or eight days. A ship, in fact, so tangibly real that it was to survive a head-on collision with an iceberg not many months after Elias Crane stood tremulously by its berth in the Liverpool docks of 1889.

He pushed through the crowds, showed his papers and arranged for his baggage to be taken on board, then embarked, descending straightaway to the second-class cabin he had reserved, to settle himself for the voyage. By the time he came back on to the teeming deck the ship was almost ready to set sail. He stared across to the solid gloom of the wharfs, his vision scored with lines of black perpendicular rain. He shivered in the bitter wind, and saw a squat warehouse transformed into the grey square tower of the church of St Mary the Virgin. Gripping the rail in the driving rain which burst from an overcast sky, he could not help but picture another morning, saturated by sunshine. Victoria would be waking; the church bells would be tolling eight o'clock. Elias saw her yawning, opening the curtains of her bedroom, to gaze on the life passing to and fro along Chapel Street. The white walls of Penzance and Newlyn would be glaring back at the sun, whilst here the relentless rain fell. Victoria would be thinking of him, perhaps she would be reading his final letter again, as above Penzance harbour seagulls cut white arcs across the blue-marbled sky of his remembrance. She would be dressing carefully, to conceal the gradual transformation in her shape, whilst the ship's funnels spun black skeins of smoke in the filthy air, and the engines began to drum out a more urgent, pounding rhythm.

Elias gripped the wet iron rail more firmly. There were shouts of farewell from those who were to be left behind on the dockside. The waving of their white handkerchiefs made the eyes of many on board spring with tears. How many of these goodbyes would last for ever, how many farewells would be said for the last time? The bell rang for breakfast in the vicarage; simultaneously, the ship's bell chimed into life. Victoria slowly descended a staircase. *The City of Rome* slid from the harbour on the swelling tide.

Elias watched the shoreline recede and finally disappear from sight in the veiling mist. On the open sea a breeze sprang up to fill the sails. The weather cleared and the ship swung westwards, skimming effortlessly over coruscating waves. Once the last extremity of land had slipped by he went below to his small cabin, to lie on his bunk, arms clasped behind his head. After a time, he became so absorbed in his own thoughts that he forgot entirely the rolling and pitching of the ship.

At length – perhaps inspired by the stability of his stomach – Elias sat up, opened his deed box and took out some sheets of writing paper. Then he settled himself at the cabin table and began to write, pausing after every sentence, his face fixed with concentration.

The Reverend Mr Southley,   The City of Rome
The Vicarage,
Chapel Street,
Penzance, England.

6th May 1889

Sir,
By the time this letter reaches you, I have no doubt that you will have learnt the very worst. Although you have every justification to deny me ~~everything~~ all forgiveness, I cannot desist from writing to express my sorrow and penitence at what has come to pass. If only I could reveal to you ~~my misery and suffering~~ one thousandth of the torments I now endure, this fraction would surely convince you of the magnitude of my entire misery and suffering

Here the pen came to a stop. Elias read what he had written, shook his head in despair and left the table. He lay down again on the bunk. He remained thus for an

175

hour, then got up and took hold of the unfinished letter as if to tear it to pieces.

But after a moment he changed his mind and replaced the sheet of paper in the deed box. As he did so, he caught sight of the photograph of the Southley family which had been taken in the garden of Holly Lodge – it seemed an eternity ago – and stared at the figure of the girl, her hair parted severely in the middle, her eyes downcast.

Chapter Twenty-Five

I find myself in a room at the Hopeville hotel in Chapel Street, Penzance, which fulfils perfectly all the seedy qualities desired by the amateur detective who has checked in to some boarding house for the sake of unravelling an unpleasant scandal. Witness the carpet: its faded green whorls of leaves are now long past their springtime; I enjoy the company of a superannuated armchair and a bow-fronted dressing-table at which I now sit to write this passage, only too aware of my own distorted reflection in its warped mirror. This dressing-table is made of some indeterminate material: it has long been disguised under thick coats of white gloss paint. Several small framed portraits of reclining cats – all too repulsive to invite their filching – adorn the mantelpiece. Thus I am ensconced in this beautiful Georgian building, amidst the results of several catastrophic house clearances.

I take my traditional English breakfast – greasy eggs, streaky bacon, tepid tinned Italian tomatoes and an equilateral triangle of cardboard masquerading as 'fried bread' – in a dungeon festooned with fishing nets and brass lanterns; salt and pepper pots are miniature lighthouses; murals of eye-patched smugglers rise all around me.

Yet from the window seat of my room, I look out at the sunlit, granite walls of the church of St Mary the

Virgin; and I have a fine aspect of Chapel Street. What matters most is that I have come to solve the mystery, and so I have explored every street in Penzance and Newlyn. I have returned to the Dolphin tavern – where my grandfather made a momentous decision to flee from England – to find it unrecognizable, even from my own youthful memories of it. Now fake portholes abound; there is reproduction Victorian furniture, an abundance of copper kettles, a plethora of decorative ropes and the apparently obligatory fishing nets; every alcove houses a model ship; from every hook swing nautical paraphernalia – lanterns, sextants, small telescopes, lobster pots; whilst fruit machines, pool tables and dartboards jostle for their places. One small sanctum of wall space retains a reproduction of an old photograph of the Dolphin, before it was ruined for the sake of the modern world, thus striking an harmonic response in me to my father's insistent lament for the decline of the old way of life into the vulgarity of the new.

For some weeks my father has been convalescing from his stroke at home, apparently making fair progress. But my stay at the Hopeville hotel is to be unexpectedly curtailed, when I receive an urgent telephone message from my mother that his condition has become critical.

I check out of the hotel at once, book my ticket to London, then wait on a bench by the appropriate platform at Penzance railway station. My thoughts are in turmoil, but suddenly, with hallucinatory clarity, I picture my grandfather standing beside me – absorbed by his own century-old misery – though, of course, his grief must arise from more extraordinary circumstances.

Chapter Twenty-Six

Some weeks after Elias Crane's departure for America, Victoria was returning to her aunt's cottage in Newlyn. She had bought fish at the harbour, and now walked, a solitary figure dressed in black, up the hill from the quayside. It was a hot summer's evening, and she passed gratefully into the shaded corridor of a narrow street. It suddenly crossed her mind that this was the street along which Elias had led her on a cold autumn night, to witness the spectacle of the packing and salting of fish. She came to the low narrow doorway through which they had passed as if into another infernal world, where ghostly faces hovered in the flaring of the lanterns. She recalled his good humour that night, his teasing of her, but beyond that his comforting presence which had seemed somehow to envelop her completely, quelling her fears. It was not simply fear of the night, or of trespassing in that dreadful place, which Elias banished; it was the fear that she would always be unhappy and isolated. She wanted to live for ever in that comforting presence.

Three men were sitting on the steps before a cottage. Victoria realized that they were watching her intently, and she hurried on. But as she did so, a voice remarked that she was Reverend Southley's daughter. Then, quite distinctly, a second voice rejoined that if it were so, the Reverend Mr Southley had tumbled a whore.

Victoria's cheeks reddened and she rushed away, fleeing the mocking laughter. She ran the rest of the way to her aunt's cottage. Once inside, she leant breathlessly against the door, tears streaming down her face.

Her aunt went to Victoria, arms outstretched, asking what was the matter, but Victoria pushed by her and threw down her basket.

'I have been spoken about . . . in the street,' she sobbed. 'They said a terible thing about my mother.'

Victoria stared angrily at her aunt, who averted her eyes and sat down very slowly. Outside the silent room a bird sang; footsteps passed by.

'Well? Am I never to be told the truth?'

Her aunt glanced at the door is if she feared she might be overheard, and spoke in a whisper.

'Please . . . do not ask this of me.'

Victoria composed herself, breathing deeply and drying her eyes.

'I was told by my "father" that I was abandoned in the graveyard. Ready for death, when I had hardly been born. But he did not say who my mother and father were, or why they left me there. That was all he told me, and that was an end to it. I never dared to ask again. It is bad enough to be tortured by this, but when people in the streets know more about me than I do myself, isn't it proper that I should know the truth?'

Her aunt remained silent.

'What was my mother's name?'

The room had grown darker. Her aunt looked up; on the verge of tears her lips looked bloodless in the dying light, and her white hands were trembling.

'Your mother's name was Mary Daniels.'

180

Victoria nodded, swallowed hard and went on in a faltering voice. 'And . . . where did she live?'

'My brother found the place, near to the harbour. It is . . . too horrible to describe.'

'And what did my mother . . . do?'

'It's said she had worked in a travelling fair.'

'Then what of my father?'

Her aunt sighed, then resolved to go on.

'My brother was told that his name was Turner. He worked on a fishing boat out of Lowestoft. He and your mother lodged in a cottage by the docks for a year or so . . . until you were born. And your father fled.'

Here she paused, then added in a voice scarcely audible: 'They had lived together out of wedlock.'

Silence fell between them; the darkness had deepened, so that neither could see the other's expression. Her aunt rose, and embraced Victoria; this wrinkled face, now wet with cold tears, seemed somehow repellent to the girl as it was pressed against her cheek. She herself shed no tears; indeed, she felt oddly unmoved by all that had been revealed to her. A sudden elation overcame her, as though someone had at last turned a key to unlock the prison of her identity. Her aunt's voice was speaking softly into her ear.

'I cannot believe how anyone could have abandoned you. You were such a beautiful child. And now you are so good, so kind, so pure. What does it matter how you came to be? Why must we break our hearts?'

Victoria withdrew from her embrace and lit the lamp upon the table.

'It is all for the best,' she said. 'I have lived as an impostor. I never was Victoria Southley. Now I shall be true to my origins.'

181

She smiled at her aunt, who returned a look of apprehension.

'I think I shall call myself Mary Turner. Yes. I shall bear my name defiantly.'

Then, as she did every evening, Victoria left the cottage and walked up the Coombe, until she reached Holly Lodge. She stood at the gate, gazing at the house, as the last rays of the sun cast the long shadows of trees across the garden. Now the flowerbeds were choked with weeds, and thistles and dandelions had burst up through the surface of the croquet lawn.

Suddenly she caught sight of a figure within, as it moved rapidly past the window. Her heart leapt. She ran down the garden path and knocked loudly at the door. She heard footsteps approaching along the hall. When the door was opened, a stranger's face greeted her.

'Is Mr Crane here?' Victoria asked in mounting confusion.

The stranger frowned.

'No,' he told her. 'Who is Mr Crane?'

'He lived here before,' she said, the sentence a cadence which traced the dying fall of her hopes. Then she learnt that this stranger had rented the property from that very morning.

Victoria mumbled her apologies and walked swiftly and purposefully away. Yet each step seemed to her to be the final pace over the edge of an abyss.

Chapter Twenty-Seven

The sea winds that blow across the tip of Cape Cod, across the endless, deserted beaches, and the vast, uninhabited tracts of heathland, fill the atmosphere of Provincetown, Massachusetts with damp salt-scented air, and strew its road with fine grey sand. The railway tracks reached here in 1873, enabling the nineteenth-century traveller to make the journey from Boston in only three or four hours. Provincetown has grown from the oldest of colonial roots, since the *Mayflower* made land here in 1662 en route to Plymouth.

The town has developed along the axis of Commercial Street, the north and south reaches of which have been named, with admirable clarity, 'Uppalong' and 'Downalong'. The nineteenth-century traveller can discover here an industrious port. From the time of the first settlers the whaling ships have set forth from this place, to return not only with cargoes of blubber and whale meat but also with a living cargo of immigrants, mainly Portuguese sailors, taken on as crew when the ships put into the Azores. These foreigners have made this place their home. So by the time the railway arrives, the Portuguese inhabitants of Provincetown have come to outnumber the native Yankees.

Each morning Elias Crane, in exile from his old world, walks along Commercial Street, the way lined with large white wooden-boarded houses, fronted by spacious verandahs. Those with whom he has dealings refer to him as 'the English gentleman painter'. But his anonymity is assured, since Provincetown is still some years away from finding itself to be a major colony for artists and a tourist attraction. By the time that the skyline has come to be dominated by the Pilgrims Memorial Monument – an architectural anachronism built in the late 1890s, but fashioned in the medieval Siennese style – there will be artists and art schools abounding.

Provincetown as a focus for artists will burgeon still more in our century, so that on the 27th of August 1916 a *Boston Sunday Globe* headline will declare this place to be 'The Biggest Art Colony in the World'. Here will also prowl a pride of literary lions – Eugene O'Neill, Edmund Wilson, Sinclair Lewis, Dos Passos. In the 1930s Jackson Pollock, Mark Rothko, Franz Kline will walk its streets and drink in its bars. In the 1950s the Atlantic, or A-House, will resound with jazz and Norman Mailer will hold court here.

In our day the population of Provincetown swells from five thousand in winter to fifty-five with the coming of summer visitors; then the streets are crowded and choked with traffic. Yet the death knell of artists' colonies was sounded long ago, in that *Boston Globe* headline. The nineteenth-century idealism which had fuelled common artistic pursuits, a shared aesthetic, a perception of grandeur in the primitive, could endure in its purest form no longer in the Provincetown of the twentieth century than it could in Barbizon, Grez, Pont-Aven or Newlyn. The essential spirit quickly fled, never to return.

*   *   *

184

But we have arrived here in May 1889, to unravel still further the life of my grandfather. For the first few months of his stay in Provincetown the novelty of his situation sustains him, and he is able to savour the freedom which his escape from England has provided. He has established himself in a cabin on the outskirts of the town, close to the sea, a place which is conducive to his desire for a reclusive life.

He begins with the best of intentions, having brought with him from Boston all the necessary materials for painting and drawing. He walks the dunes and heathlands every day, searching for scenes to sketch. From time to time he sends letters to his father, in which he lies consummately about his circumstances.

Through the summer months he lives cheaply, even supplementing the money he has by labouring occasionally at the docks, where work is plentiful. But as autumn sets in his moods begin to darken. Now he feels consumed by loneliness, and an impending event throws a perpetual shadow across his mind. For by the year's end he will have become a father. So each morning he walks along Commercial Street with a single objective: to buy a bottle of whisky, which he will spend the day consuming. His ability to work dissolves, so that the days are spent sitting on his verandah, staring across the monotonous dunes towards the sea, his thoughts devoured by remorse.

Elias now realized that in the feverish activity which preceded his flight he had been solely concerned with where, and by what means, his new existence would take place, and not with the question of whether he would be able to live with his conscience. So the ramifications of his impulsive actions slowly uncoiled in his mind. He saw Victoria cast out of the Southley household. Then how would she live, and how would she be able to bear her shame? His absorption in his own fate had blinded him to hers. But now he saw her condemned to the workhouse, forced to wear the yellow badge of shame as an unmarried mother. In his mind she raised her skirts for strangers on filthy beds in squalid rooms. Even at best he envisaged her in some futile existence of hardship and drudgery, always burdened by the child he had given her. Beyond this he was forced to acknowledge that he had deluded himself that he had never loved her. Yet he had set a trap for himself which he could not evade, for he could not return to her; he would never be able to make amends.

So the seasons of 1890 unravelled to bring us to the winter of the year. On a December morning, as a gale swept flurries of rain off the sea to rattle on the cabin roof, my grandfather walked into Provincetown, bought a bottle of whisky and picked up a letter from his mother, which was waiting for his collection at the poste restante. It told him that his father was dead, that the funeral service had been held some two weeks before. When Elias returned to his cabin later that morning he was carrying two parcels wrapped in brown paper. He laid them on the table, took out the bottle of whisky from the first and half filled a glass. Then he sat down and unwrapped the gun he had just purchased.

The gun weighed heavily in his hands, yet still it seemed like some childhood toy. His father had kept a collection of weapons and would polish them each

Sunday morning, allowing no other hands to touch them. Elias's thoughts rushed back to his boyhood. He felt again the utter powerlessness which had always overwhelmed him in his father's presence. He remembered the strangeness of those old disciplinary rituals – how he had marched upon a square of carpet to barked commands, and how his small fingers had been crushed in the vice of the bronze hand. To have been forced to respect what he loathed, to fear where he should have loved, to have grown up to be lonely and secretive, with always an unnameable chill of dread about his heart – he saw how all these things had conspired to make him what he was. And now he was a man, still he was powerless to shape his own fate.

He broke open the gun and dropped three bullets into alternate spaces in the chamber. Then he spun the chamber and snapped the gun shut, drained his glass and went outside.

Is a winter sky of ivory clouds, streaming across a pale red sun, to be the last sky my grandfather sees? Are swollen raindrops hurled on the fast Atlantic wind, dropping like tiny bombs, to be the last which fall upon his living face? He walks along the deserted shoreline. Out to sea a whaling vessel is beating against the rollers; on the strand the waves collapse with deafening detonations. Elias sits down at the edge of the dunes. The damp grey sand sticks to his hands, and he wipes them on his jacket, then takes the gun from his pocket. The barrel rests against his temple, but his hand is shaking and he changes his mind. He must make certain, so he puts the barrel to his lips. The cold kiss of the gun-metal shocks him, but he grips it between his teeth. His thumb presses upon the trigger, and the chamber begins to revolve, fraction by fraction. Suddenly he tears the gun from his mouth, gasping for air. He gets unsteadily to his feet, takes aim and fires. A loud report and the bullet flies into a distant breaking wave. The wind snatches the absurd sound of laughter from his throat. Then he hurls the gun high into the air and watches it plummet, like a dark, wheeling bird, into the sea.

Three hours later, Elias is riding on a train bound for Boston.

Chapter Twenty-Eight

My father used to laugh in the face of extinction. In between the times of his confinements in hospital, he would fantasize about the possible modes of his own death and burial. Over lunch he might settle for a modest pyramid, to be erected in the back garden, with perhaps a couple of old ex-schoolteaching colleagues to be sacrificially slaughtered, to keep him company in the afterlife. He would propose next door's cat as a suitable candidate for mummification. Over dinner he might favour a Viking funeral – to be cast adrift on a burning longship, launched at sunset from the slipway beside his favourite riverside pub in Richmond. One distinct advantage of this method, he would point out to me, would be that all his relatives and friends could enjoy the spectacle from the comfort of the lounge bar: his floating bier would sink sizzlingly into the Thames, leaving a most picturesque cloud of whirling blue woodsmoke.

As his coffin rolled, with angry-sounding thunder, out of sight, and scarlet curtains were drawn in its wake, I could not help but feel that I had failed him somehow. At least he had ended in fierce, cleansing fire, whilst outside the frozen earth lay dead under a deep fall of snow.

The mourners filed out of the church. Black cars stood tombstone-dark in a pure white world, waiting to convey us slowly home to tea, sandwiches, and the unwanted reminiscences of ex-colleagues and distant relatives, whose faces I hardly recognized.

So ended a week in which I felt I had moved through an icy dream of unreality. And I had pondered the ironies when my mother and I went to register his death, according to cold clerical procedure, at a modern council office – one so utterly unremarkable in every way that it remains unforgettable in every detail. For it was there that my father entered the lists of those he had endeavoured for so long to live amongst, now taking his place in that boundless realm of dead facts, an eternal imprisonment in official records.

Chapter Twenty-Nine

As a locomotive of the Great Western Railway drew into Penzance station, the late December afternoon of 1890 saw a high sea and a cold wind driving clouds of spray on to the deserted promenade. My grandfather's footsteps carried him from the station into Market Jew Street, where a quick glance to right and left satisfied him that, between the three boarding houses within his field of vision, there could be little to choose. He therefore entered the nearest establishment – the Ocean Rest House – and secured a modest but comfortable room.

The landlord brought him a jug of cold water and a bowl, and Elias set about refreshing himself, although he could not wash his mind and body free of the states of anxiety and exhaustion into which they had been increasingly driven.

The Atlantic crossing, in heavy winter storms, had proved more fearful than he could ever have imagined, with any object which was not securely bolted to floors, walls or ceilings assuming a life of violent and unpredictable motion. Elias returned bruised, weary from lack of sleep, and feeble from a nausea which had prevented him from eating for days at a time, to the blessed calm of the Liverpool dockside.

From there he had hurried to the family home in Cheshire, in order to deposit the belongings with which he had returned from America, and to spend a little time with his mother. Together they visited his father's grave, by which his mother wept uncontrollably, whilst he made a pretence of grief, but experienced no stirring of his emotions. After two nights spent at the farmhouse he felt that he could prevaricate no longer, and set off on the journey to Penzance, though the prospect of what lay ahead of him filled him with anguish.

As night fell outside his room in the Ocean Rest House, he contemplated his strategy, determining that on the following morning he would send a brief note to request an urgent audience with the Reverend Mr Southley, asking for a reply by return. He sat down at the dressing-table in his room to compose this note, but quickly discarded it as soon as he realized that he could have no control over Reverend Southley's response. The note might be disdainfully ignored, or might provoke some furious reply. He saw lawyers at the boarding-house door, demanding entrance to serve him writs of breach of promise. Such eventualities had to be avoided at all costs. The more he pondered the predicament, the more he saw that his most effective ploy lay in coming to Reverend Southley unexpectedly, in order that he might catch him off his guard, and so use the opportunity to plead his penitence and pledge his desire to make amends. It would be an approach which harboured its own perils, yet he was unable to see a better way.

For the rest of that night sleep eluded him entirely. He felt no desire to take any dinner and merely asked the landlord to fetch him a jug of cider, which he rapidly vanquished. Afterwards he lay on his bed, sipping at a hip flask of whisky, hoping to dull his senses, craving that oblivion would claim him soon. Yet with each burning mouthful intractable problems seemed to become more magnified, and insuperable difficulties sprang up in his mind with ever more dispiriting clarity.

Dawn broke, cold and misty. With the intensifying of the light Market Jew Street began to assume solidity, waking into life as pony carts rattled by, voices greeted each other, and the first train to London declaimed its departure in bursts of clamorous energy, its wheels spinning madly on the frost-glazed rails. All signified to Elias the return of an unbearable reality.

Then an infant began to howl in some adjacent room, and he could tolerate the freezing confines of his own no longer. He washed his face and hands, donned his hat and cloak, and set out into that familiar yet foreign world.

It was now past seven o'clock, and yet an hour too early to make the call for which he had journeyed halfway across the world. Instead, he decided to walk along the promenade to Newlyn. The wind had abated and the sound of the sea was muted, as though it had been suffocated under the gigantic cauldron of mist which filled Mount's Bay. But Elias did not care to behold the world, only to walk and to walk, that he might burn off the restless energy which drove him blindly towards an unknown destiny.

At the Coombe, he paused on the bridge. Here the mist thickened and swirled, whilst below the stream's incessant voices passed by, on their way to be lost in the sea. He was alone on the lane as he climbed the hill, whilst the bare dripping trees, which intertwined their boughs above him, clattered with the falling of dew.

When he reached Holly Lodge, its outlines were scarcely visible from the garden gate. Though he walked a little way up the lane, the glasshouse was entirely obscured by the mist. A vision of Victoria – naked, her black hair streaming about her as she spun round, her body so white, almost insubstantial – surged into his mind, and made him turn away, slowly to retrace his steps back to Penzance.

As Elias passed by the Dolphin tavern and started up the steep ascent of Quay Street, the clock tower of the Church of St Mary resounded with the tolling of eight o'clock. The structure dwarfed him as he reached the beginning of Chapel Street. Suddenly he felt as if he would faint; after his long walk the cold seemed to have pierced to the heart of him, and he leant against the wall of the church, his teeth chattering and his body trembling.

Now it was time to admit to himself that he had come as far as he could, that ultimately he had no spirit for this. After all, he had been free in America; and he need never forsake that liberation in England. Neither Reverend Southley nor Victoria had succeeded in tracing him to his family home. Then why should he forfeit his life?

The vicarage lay before him, its windows in darkness; no-one was approaching along Chapel Street. Elias turned on his heels.

At that moment the loud shrill crying of a seagull, perched high upon some invisible rooftop, sounded along the empty street. Its high-pitched calls seemed at once like some demoniacal laughter, or some unearthly scream of desolation. Into Elias's mind flooded an absurd, incomprehensible memory. He was a boy of fourteen or fifteen years old, sitting at a wooden desk, in a classroom filled with bronze light. The teacher was reciting an ancient poem, translating each verse into modern English. The poem – which now unravelled haphazardly in his mind, phrases and fragments jostling together – was called 'The Seafarer'. It had been composed in an age which had ended so long ago that Elias's young imagination had been incapable of conceiving the gulf which separated it from his own world. But he remembered that the seafarer's destiny had been that of an outcast. He pictured the Anglo-Saxon word, written in stark white letters upon a blackboard: 'WRAECCA'. An exile. A man who – Elias could not remember what crime he had committed – had been banished from his way of life, and severed from all earthly joys. And so the seafarer was fated to be alone for ever, his only company the beating of waves on alien shores, the wind-driven snow, and the forlorn cries of seabirds.

My grandfather mounted the steps under the high portico of the vicarage. He took a deep breath, cleared his throat, then pulled the bell-rope. A remote ringing sounded within; Elias's heart hammered in his ears. The door was opened, fraction by excruciating fraction, to reveal an elderly housekeeper, dressed in a starched white cap and apron. He could not be sure if he remembered her from his former visits.

'I am Elias Crane,' he announced, with a surprising sureness of tone. 'I should like to speak to the Reverend Mr Southley.'

The woman's brow furrowed, and her mouth formed a perfect, wrinkled O.

'I'm afraid that's not possible, sir,' she countered, folding her arms decisively.

'But it is of the most crucial importance that he should see me,' Elias protested, glancing anxiously past her into the dark hallway.

The housekeeper leant forward towards him, whispering conspiratorially.

'You can't see him, sir,' she said in a low voice, shaking her head emphatically, 'because Reverend Southley's gone to a better place.'

'You mean a new diocese?'

Now she shook her head yet more vigorously, pointed in the direction of the graveyard, then preposterously thrust up her index finger towards the supernal sky.

'He is dead?' Elias said, incredulously.

She nodded solemnly.

'Then what of Mrs Southley? And the children?' exclaimed Elias in amazement.

'Mrs Southley went her husband's way. A good half-year ago. And the children went to his sister's, away in Newlyn.'

Elias nodded in bewilderment, thanked the housekeeper, and descended the steps, unable to assimilate these shocking disclosures into his expectations.

The door to the church stood open, and desiring only peace and solitude in which to ponder these unforeseen developments, Elias stepped inside, walking slowly towards the altar, his footsteps resounding and his breath billowing around him in the chill air. He had never before ventured within these granite walls, and although it is possible that Reverend Southley had described the history of the church to him, it is doubtful that he could have recalled it then, or that it mattered in the least to him that he could not. But Mary's Chapel had stood on this site from 1549, and so had lent its name to Chapel Street. The building of this newer church, in the early Gothic style, had been completed in 1835, and its consecration had been admitted in 1836. The use of granite, in Commissioner's Perpendicular, represented then, as now, a superior and imposing work of Georgian architecture in Cornwall.

But such aesthetic considerations were far from Elias's mind. Indeed, the massive weight of the Church of St Mary's structure seemed to oppress him further, and the dank air and sepulchral interior soon drove him out into Chapel Street once more.

He made his way down to the promenade and took a place on a bench facing the sea, pulling his cloak more tightly around him. He took out the hip flask of whisky in which a single mouthful remained, swallowed it, then concentrated on his divided thoughts. Whilst he was shocked by the deaths of Reverend Southley and his wife, he could see at once that such a turn of events was wholly fortuitous from the point of view of his own predicament. At the same time, he could not begin to guess at its consequences for Victoria. Perhaps she had run away by now; perhaps she had even found a husband or a lover, a man capable of disregarding the shame which he had heaped upon her. Whatever the case might be, he had penetrated too far into the mystery to leave it unresolved.

By now a breeze, borne on the incoming tide, had begun to disperse the mist. Elias made his way slowly towards Newlyn, for the second time that morning. At the corner of Chywoone Hill, a man whom he recognized – a fellow painter from his former Newlyn days –

passed by him. Elias quickened his pace, fearful of recognition, but the man walked on, staring straight ahead, apparently lost in his own thoughts.

Elias stopped at the corner of Old Paul Hill and gazed up the steep cobbled street towards the cottage, which stood a mere twenty paces away. Still he felt transfixed by indecision and remained at this draughty vantage point. Passers-by eyed the stranger with suspicion, and he was on the point of fleeing their scrutiny when a figure emerged from the low door of the cottage. He was as certain as he could be, after the passing of nineteen months, that this elderly lady was the Reverend Mr Southley's sister. She approached the corner at which Elias was standing; he turned his back to her, and she went by without lifting her gaze from the cobblestones, then passed out of sight.

Even now Elias made no move towards the cottage. He was still pacing up and down, summoning his courage, when the cottage door was opened again and the figure of a boy ran out into the street. This time Elias had no difficulty in identifying a taller and a broader Abraham, as he raced down the hill towards him. Elias suddenly stepped out to block his swift progress, and the boy skidded to a halt a few feet away.

'Your name is Abraham, is it not?'

The boy's eyes flashed with panic, revealing no trace of recognition. He merely saw a stranger, a man attired in a black cloak and tall silk hat, who towered threateningly above him. He could hardly be blamed for this failure, since the face he beheld had changed absolutely. Now it was thinner, with pinched cheeks, a sallow complexion, and dark staring eyes, wide with trepidation.

'Don't you remember me?' Elias asked, as Abraham retreated a pace.

'My name is Elias Crane.'

The boy frowned, and stared in disquietude at this unfamiliar face. Then his expression was gradually transformed into one of joyful recognition.

'Mr Crane!' he shouted excitedly. 'You've come back! I said you'd come back! She wouldn't believe me, but I told her so. I asked about you every day until she shouted at me that you were dead, and that I should never speak your name again. But I didn't believe her. You're not a ghost, are you?'

Elias laughed. 'No, I'm not a ghost.'

Then, abruptly, he seized Abraham by the hand and led him around the corner into a narrow alleyway. Elias crouched down before the boy, so that their eyes were level.

'Then you have not thrown yourself into any more rivers?'

Abraham giggled and shook his head.

'Now listen to me carefully. This is very important. Does your sister live with you in the cottage?'

'Of course,' he replied. 'She's at home now.'

Elias took a deep breath and closed his eyes. Then he slowly stood up.

'Come, then. You had better take me to see her.'

Abraham led the way to the door of the cottage. He flung it open and ran inside, whilst Elias faltered on the threshold, peering into the small dimly-lit room: to the right, an oak table; to the left a dresser; a stone floor; on the far wall a clock and some framed pictures; a mantelpiece, cluttered with ornaments; below it, a hearth with a newly-kindled fire burning. The green wood hissed and spluttered, sending whorls of pale blue smoke up the chimney. To one side of the fire, with her back to the door, sat Victoria.

She looked around upon Abraham's entrance. For a fraction of a second her eyes met Elias's, before she quickly returned her gaze to the fire.

'He's come back!' cried Abraham suddenly.

Elias removed his hat, stepped inside the cottage and closed the door behind him.

'I told you he would!' Abraham was shouting triumphantly. 'Told you so! Told you so!'

Elias murmured her name whilst Abraham danced around behind him, holding on to his cloak.

Then she spoke. But it was not to Elias.

'Abraham,' she said firmly, 'go out now.'

It was the very deadness of her tone which brought the boy's capering to a halt. He gave her a puzzled stare, then looked desperately towards Elias for some contradiction of the command. But the man whom he had deified, as his hero and saviour, nodded slowly in concordance with it. So Abraham obeyed, slipping noiselessly from the room, tears welling into his eyes.

Now Elias stood alone, awkwardly, in the middle of that small room, fighting within himself for some fitting phrase to deliver.

'I have come back.' He could find no other words.

Victoria did not reply, nor did she spare him the briefest of glances.

'I have come back,' he announced, with greater resolution, 'to make amends.'

Still she did not respond. He took a few paces towards her. Her hair was gathered in a bun, exposing the nape of her neck, and he was overcome by a powerful urge to brush his lips against the pale skin.

'I have returned to ask your forgiveness.'

She shook her head slowly. Elias moved alongside her, closer to the fire, so that he could study her profile in the glow of the flames.

'I know you cannot forgive me now, at this very moment,' he continued, but was cut short by a more vigorous shaking of her head.

Elias took a deep breath, trying to suppress the exasperation which welled in his thoughts. He bent towards her, his voice falling to a whisper.

'Do you imagine that I am blind to the fact that I brought nothing but shame to you and your family?'

Suddenly her eyes darted to his.

'Shame?' she echoed mockingly. 'I had no sense of shame. Only of *betrayal*.'

Her voice lingered, almost lovingly, on the final word.

Elias began to pace around the room, marshalling his thoughts.

'Very well. Perhaps *you* felt no shame . . . but for your family . . .'

Her voice was heavy with weariness, as though she were attempting to explain a matter of utter simplicity to a slow-witted child.

'No, there was no shame for them, since they never knew what we . . . were to each other.'

Elias stopped in his tracks and stared at her; she remained immobile, gazing into the flames.

'But how so?' he exclaimed incredulously. 'What of the child? You could hardly have kept that secret from them.'

Victoria remained silent. At once Elias realized, with a great surge of hope, what had come to pass.

'I see!' he went on. 'So the child was lost to you without their knowing. Then surely we are saved!'

At that moment he would have crossed the room and taken Victoria in his arms, had he not been frozen by the startling sound of her laughter.

'The child was not lost to me,' she replied scornfully. 'How on earth could it have been, since I never was with child!'

Outside, daylight seemed to wane; Elias saw a dissolving darkness gather around him. Only the fire resisted it, hurling the broken shadows of chairs and tables against the walls; beside its brightness, her silhouetted form seemed blackest of all. This blackness filled his mind, blinding him with amazement. He stood, like a man gazing at a night sky, his powers of understanding rendered helpless and absurd in the face of infinity and eternity.

'Never with child?' he whispered.

'I never was with child,' she repeated.

In the silence, the fire settled, and a shower of blue sparks streamed up the chimney.

'Then . . . you deceived me.'

'You *betrayed* me.'

Elias's rage burst from him.

'You mean to say that you wilfully deceived me!' he shouted. 'That I have exiled myself to the other side of the world for all this time – and for nothing! For a mad idea in the head of an idiotic young girl!'

Now Victoria rose to her feet and turned to face him, her body taut and her fists clenched, though her voice did not waver when she spoke.

'I deceived you out of love for you, whilst you betrayed me out of love for yourself. Perhaps it was a test. Perhaps I meant to test your love. Whatever drove me to it – you failed me dreadfully.'

'Then you are surely insane!' Elias cried. 'For what

possible good could have come from this ridiculous idea?'

Victoria sat down again by the fire.

'You were the sole source of happiness in my life, the sole hope I had of escaping from this place, and my own misery. I knew that you would not stay here for ever. And I did not want you to leave without me. I gave myself to you because of that. But you betrayed my trust.'

Elias felt that his legs would no longer support him; he reached out to steady himself against the table.

'I can scarcely believe what I hear,' he murmured. 'It is unbearable to me.'

For a few moments, no words were exchanged. His fury abated, as all thoughts and utterances now fell apart before they could be formed. He looked out of the narrow window, but found no inspiration in the prospect of the shabby cottages opposite, nor in the strip of glowering sky beneath which they crouched.

'Listen to me,' he said at length. 'We must be calm. I have come back here to make amends. Although I am dismayed by your revelations, we may still salvage something from this.'

He moved closer to Victoria and placed his hand lightly upon her shoulder; instantly she shrugged herself free of his touch.

'Let us forget what has happened,' he implored her. 'Let us simply eradicate the past and then begin afresh. Once that is done, there can be no impediment to our beginning a new life together.'

'No impediment?' she scoffed. 'I deceived you. You betrayed me. I would count those faults as two impodiments to this new life together. No, it cannot be.'

'So . . . I am to take this as your final decision?'

At this moment the cottage door opened and Victoria's aunt entered. Seeing a stranger in the gloom before her, she let out a cry of surprise and alarm.

'Who is this gentleman?' she asked sternly of Victoria.

Elias, composing himself, stepped forward quickly.

'My name is Elias Crane,' he informed her. 'We met before, a long time ago. I brought Abraham back to you, after he had fallen into the flood at the Coombe. Do you remember me?'

'Why, of course!' she exclaimed suddenly. 'How pleasant to see you again. You were a friend of my brother's, I recall. But did you not leave Newlyn very suddenly?'

'I . . . had to travel abroad at short notice.'

'Then you must stay to tea, and let us have all your news.'

'It is kind of you, but I must very shortly catch the train for London,' Elias rejoined hastily. 'I simply came to pay my respects, and to offer my condolences for Reverend Southley's sad death.'

Before he could be detained any longer Elias snatched his hat from the table, and bade goodbye to her.

Once he stepped out into the chill air, Elias found that he had been sweating profusely, and he took out a handkerchief to mop his brow. He hurried up Chywoone Hill, then – heedless of his direction, desiring only to put some distance between himself and the cottage – he turned down a narrow alleyway. For a short time he was lost amidst unfamiliar courtyards, but went on like a sleepwalker, until he glimpsed the sea below and emerged at last at the harbour.

Elias's fate, then – so completely unforeseen, so ironically engineered – was to be granted his freedom, after all. This fate came as a dreadful revelation, bringing no consolation whatsoever to his soul. For he had returned to England armed at last with the moral and mental courage to overcome all the painful wrongs he had caused to others, and fully prepared to bear all his responsibilities, no matter how weighty they might prove. From the moment he had placed the barrel of a gun to his head, on a rainswept beach near Provincetown, Elias had known that he could not face death, and so would have to face life. Thus he had found the strength to continue the struggle, rather than step into oblivion. Yet he had declared war on a host of phantoms. The noblest decision of his life had ended in a vacuous gesture. Love, he knew, had been forfeited, with no grounds remaining for it to be reclaimed. And this destiny laughingly denied him the redemption of his self-respect.

So he walked back to Penzance, those three still incomprehensible words burning intolerably in his brain: 'Never with child . . .'

Elias is now standing before the façade of Oppenheim's Great Furnishing Mart in Market Jew Street. We see him enter and converse briefly with an old, bald-headed retainer, who sets to working out some elaborate computation of payment due, with much scratching at the shrubs of coarse grey hair which flank his face. At long last he disappears into the depths of cellars and storerooms, emerging triumphantly some minutes later to restore a small number of items to their owner.

Now Elias has nothing to detain him in Cornwall. He returns to the Ocean Rest House, lays a parcel wrapped in sacking upon his bed and carefully unties it. The painting entitled 'Golden Rules' stares back into its creator's mind. To Elias, an age seems to have passed since he made the painting. If he had finished the work yesterday, he would loathe it today; but now it appears to him as a curious relic, the work of an unknown hand, of a man who inhabited some other, happier world that has long since perished. And so he studies it, feeling somewhat uneasy and perplexed, before he wraps it up again.

Elias sits at the small dressing-table, considering his own reflection. Then, compelled to do what his reason resists, he takes a sheet of paper and a pen. He writes a sentence, then begins another, then stops suddenly. He tears the paper in half, throws away what he has composed and writes four brief lines on the remaining half-page. He seals this in an envelope, then addresses and stamps it. At the station he posts the letter, then boards the train for London.

Chapter Thirty

Let my grandfather speed from Penzance to London, courtesy of the Great Western Railway, whilst I sit in my study, attempting to visualize the kind of world to which he is returning. I conjecture that, after the Bohemian life he has lived in artists' colonies in France, Cornwall and America, London of a century ago is probably as alien a territory to him as it is to me. So I propose that, for a short while, we should live parallel lives, a hundred years apart.

He intends to spend a day or two in the capital before returning to the family home in Cheshire. So where he goes I, too, shall follow; and thus we shall have the opportunity, as it were, to compare notes. For, although the movable scenery of the city may have changed to greater or lesser degrees, it is largely recognizable after this hundred-year space; and although the details of how we live now have been altered through time, the general conditions and characteristics of life have not.

As he emerged from Paddington station, my grandfather felt at once that he was being sucked inexorably into the imploded life of the metropolis. He walked along a crowded street over which the yellow fog of daylight appeared to have solidified halfway up the towers of the Great Western Hotel, so that the world seemed to be imprisoned under this oppressive sky, its streets clouded with the smoke of some modern-day inferno. Dislocated scenes and images flowed by him – noisy news-vendors and insistent beggars, ginger cake and hot-chestnut sellers, advertisements for Reid's essense of coffee and Thunder Clouds tobacco.

During those years spent remotely in rural England, France and America, he had strayed far from this new world, and had forgotten the bewildering complexity of the city. It seemed now to crowd in upon his innocence with frightening intensity. In an attempt to distance himself a little from it he boarded a horse-drawn omnibus. He gazed at the now accelerated cosmorama of London with perhaps a vestige of the amazement, curiosity and fear experienced by a South Pacific islander, on catching his first glimpse of a great eighteenth-century sailing ship beating into shore.

Of this social labyrinth, and the multitude of miseries and injustices it harboured, Elias knew next to nothing. He had wilfully diverted the stream of history away from his mind, so that he was blissfully unaware that serious riots had taken place in Trafalgar Square and the West End in 1886 and 1887, or that unemployment – a word first formally used in social economics in the previous year – affected over a quarter of London's working men. He was oblivious to the growing organization of labour, to the concept of strikes, and would have been amazed to learn that dockers had recently withdrawn their services for a month – financed in this action by other trade unions as far afield as Australia, whence £30,000 was provided – in order that they might secure the rate of six pence an hour for their work. My grandfather was, of course, unaware of the existence of Friedrich Engels –

who was particularly gratified by the results of the dock strike – or of Karl Marx, and had no idea that *The Communist Manifesto* was available in an English edition.

The notion of class struggle would have been incomprehensible to my grandfather, for he would never have paused to consider the true reality of late nineteenth-century England – a country rich in land-owners and manufacturers, which could never claim the status of a true democracy. No woman could vote, and a third of adult men were unenfranchised because they were the recipients of poor relief, or were lodgers or domestic servants, or because they were forced to follow itinerant occupations.

I follow Elias from the Charing Cross Hotel along the Strand, which is jammed with vehicles and Christmas shoppers. He stands on the far side of the road from the West Strand Improvements building, the creation of Nash in 1830. The block is surmounted by two 'pepper-pot' towers. My grandfather stands in a crowd, staring upwards to the top of one of these towers, to witness a strange phenomenon. The Electric Time Signal Ball – a zinc sphere, six feet in diameter – is raised by pneumatic pressure, ascending the pole which is its axis, until it attains a height one hundred and twenty-nine feet above the level of the river Thames. Then, at precisely one o'clock Greenwich Mean Time, a burst of current transmitted along a direct cable from the Observatory causes the sphere to fall suddenly for ten feet. People adjust their pocket watches and pass on . . .

Walking in his footsteps takes me to the mid-point of the Strand. Where I see a tie shop, a travel agency, he sees the entrance to the Tivoli music-hall theatre. He enters and buys a dark sweet beer at the bar, contemplates the possibility of entering the auditorium to watch a matinée performance, but is discouraged by the thought that a man in a bad humour ought not to expose himself to the risk of adding to his store.

He finishes his drink and goes out again into the street. As he walks up to Covent Garden, his eye is caught by a hoarding on a wall. It advertises the glories of the Crystal Palace, not only as a wonder of the modern world, but because the area is 'Exceptionally Healthy due to Prevailing Winds from the Coast'. He is further informed that it stands '380 Feet Above Thames – Therefore out of the Valley of Fogs: The Fresh Air Suburb'. With London crowds, pollution and traffic all assailing his senses, he resolves that he will escape there for the afternoon. Then he will return to sleep at the Charing Cross Hotel, catch the train back to Cheshire the following morning, and never set foot in London again.

Sitting alone on a bench, his cloak wrapped tightly around him against the fitful bursts of bitter air, my grandfather enjoys an unimpeded view across a wide ornamental lake with twin fountains, over the terrace with its broad flight of steps, still further to the more distant balustrade, topped by statues spaced equidistantly, on beyond the trees, to the melting outline of the Crystal Palace. The building seems to hang majestically in the winter air, between the twin Italianate water towers designed by Brunel: perfect in its symmetry – although it is no longer, since a fire destroyed its eastern transept, which was never to be rebuilt, a quarter of a century before – for my grandfather's imagination restores it to wholeness.

Perhaps the long-dead Joseph Mallory – hat-maker of Ditton – would find in this spectacle the most fitting symbol of the new spirit of the age about which he dreamt, for here industry and art are combined in glass and wood, iron and stone, to form this most beautiful artifice.

If Elias were now to turn around he would see spread before him a panorama of Kentish countryside, across which lights are being lit in streets and houses, to herald the coming of the dusk. He would be able to see, at the foot of the hill, the site where men are laying the foundations of a building. In this house his grandson, whom he will never know, will one day write these words. This grandson will never be able to walk up the hill without seeing a phantom palace of glass hanging in the air, nor survey those landscaped grounds without lamenting that the terraces have crumbled, the flights of steps have collapsed, that only here and there stand decapitated statues silhouetted against the sky, whilst others are overturned and heaped together, spent by time and vandalism – mythological figures, broken and limbless, cast into their communal graves.

Darkness is falling. But Elias is not contemplating the ruins of time, only those of his own life. He cannot foresee the great fire of 1936 – in which glass melts, iron buckles, wood becomes ashes and stone crumbles – forever to deprive his grandson of the marvel he has witnessed. Nor does he realize that I am at his side as he rises from the bench, and that I walk with him around the lake and up the wide flight of steps; that we pass, shoulder to shoulder, between the gigantic sphinx-like figures hewn from granite which flank the exit from this imperilled palace; that my voice is in his ear, urging him to return to London, then to Cheshire, because I cannot bear his loneliness and grief for much longer, and because I think I know how to set him free.

Chapter Thirty-One

She had wrung its neck – decapitated, plucked, gutted, stuffed, dressed and roasted the lifeless torso of this bird – so that it might, by its death, give the culminating performance of its life. But now it seemed to crouch miserably – almost apologetically – on a silver platter in the centre of the dining table, its white bones exposed here and there by the stripping of its cadaverous, textured flesh, its life casually forfeited in the cause of a Christmas dinner which neither the mother who had prepared it, nor the son who had travelled two hundred miles to contemplate it, could stomach. They had picked at various parts of its carcass, but he now pushed the remnants of his meal aside, whilst she drenched hers with tears which streamed down her cheeks, cascaded from her chin, and dripped, like water from a melting icicle, from the tip of her nose.

'He was a good man,' she declaimed hoarsely. 'He might have been here today if *you* hadn't failed him. He had the highest hopes of you. All gone to waste. Look at you – you! – daring to come back without a penny! So now it comes to this!'

Elias remained in rigid silence, his eyes fixed on the dismal sight of his half-eaten plate of food. In that miniature landscape, between the mauled hummocks of meat, roast potatoes and parsnips, lay congealing ponds of gravy in which the fat had begun to coalesce like small silver-white globules of mercury.

For a few moments his mother composed herself, dabbing at her eyes with a blue lace handkerchief.

Her speech resumed, further down the scale.

'Your father left some money to me. But it will scarcely suffice, since you tell me you have none at all. So I have been forced to decide to sell off most of our land.'

'What!' Elias exclaimed, starting to his feet. 'But that is a ridiculous idea. The land's hardly worth anything!'

His mother also rose from her seat.

'Then I had better fetch you the letter from the railway company which intends to purchase it.'

Elias read it in silence, with mounting horror, then handed it back to her without comment.

'Oh, don't be alarmed, dear boy,' she said, answering his look of trepidation with a sardonic tone. 'You shall have some money to invest. And yes, you may continue to live here. But I am going to move to my sister's. I am going to Chester – to die!'

Elias put on his cloak and went outside. He walked across the cobbled yard, round by the derelict barn and out into the open fields. Cold, pure air gusted about him, bringing with it fitful showers of snow, which alighted on the blades of grass and instantly dissolved, like a million tiny white stars extinguished. Towards the horizon gaunt trees stood black against the clouded alabaster of the sky. He walked on, far across the deserted fields, lost in contemplation.

He saw it all clearly in his imagination. The future rushed towards him as swiftly and thunderously as a locomotive. So even here, lost in the countryside, the trains would one day hurtle by, leaving behind them acrid trails of filthy smoke. And the steam and the smoke and the noise would say: 'We are the new world. We are racing over your closed horizons, and we shall have our day.' He saw the gangs of navvies, levelling the path of the track, laying the wooden sleepers, unloading the iron rails, building embankments and erecting fences. Then he saw houses, factories, warehouses conjured out of the air, to obliterate these fields and to fell the copses of trees. He turned and looked back at the ancient house in the distance. Long before it had lived out its natural existence he saw it torn apart, and fancied he heard it scream in some inanimate agony of demolition. If only he could freeze the time-wave of his world! These fields and woods had been the sole solace of his unhappy upbringing, and he wandered along, tracing the boundary of the land, an anxious king in an imperilled domain, as the loss of yet another ideal made him turn his blind hatred upon his age.

Within the month his mother had departed for Chester, leaving Elias to an absolute solitude, the potential enjoyment of which was to be postponed for some while, since he fully intended to extract his pound of flesh from the modern world.

Thus he was visited by a battalion of fawning railway company officials and a phalanx of sycophantic lawyers. Deeds were pored over, maps consulted, prices per acre earnestly debated for hours upon end. Elias refused offer after offer, stubbornly forcing up the price. For he possessed all the time in the world and the secure knowledge that the railway simply could not be built without the possession of his family's lands. With malicious glee he watched those emissaries of the future despair and go away wringing their hands to consult the greedy investors, then return the following day with newly improved terms.

By the spring the matter was settled, and Elias made safe investments from the capital he had gained, which would ensure – at least on paper – that he need never have to take up any occupation to earn his living. It was a victory, though one tinged with bitterness.

Now he might have begun to paint again, yet he had lost all inclination. Now he might have travelled with the furious energy and enthusiasm of a man in flight from himself. Yet he could not, for he had stared into the mirror of self-loathing for too long. With all illusions stripped away, he had been left with only the intolerable reality: that his was a mind of mediocre talents; and that his was a character woven from second-hand threads. He was a patchwork man, who had lacked the courage to embrace death, yet had failed to master life. And so, as his loneliness and isolation deepened, he saw before him only endless stretches of uneventful time.

But the imagination which had looked, with visionary clarity, upon those houses, factories and warehouses rising out of the land around him, had not foreseen a summer's morning when he would return from sketching desultorily in the fields, to encounter a figure standing by his garden gate, staring questioningly at the house.

Elias stopped in his tracks, then went slowly onwards, to greet the woman who was to become his wife and bear him his first son.

Part Three

Chapter Thirty-Two

Sit down with me, in my father's study. Here things are still as they were in the beginning. You may think it morbid that this place is unchanged, that the magnifying glass, the dusty books, the dog-eared papers and the files piled high are unmoved, enshrined, Miss Havisham-ed (without the cobwebs and the wedding cake). There is the cork notice board, to which are pinned sepia-tinted photographs, addresses, telephone numbers, reminders to himself to check such and such a date, or to obtain such and such a book, before the time to do these things ran out.

The ancient leather armchairs are comfortable. Perhaps we have had a good dinner; perhaps we are enjoying a glass of decent port or brandy. Perhaps we can forget for a while that a television or a radio in another room could be telling us that the world we live in is full of unbearable horrors. Perhaps, instead, we can consider a possible version of events, take stock of how far we have come with our story, and consider where it must lead; create – as my father loved to do – lives from lifeless facts.

Study a photograph on the desk before us. It is small, oval, silver-framed. There is the face of the son born to Elias Crane and Victoria Southley, who had chosen to call herself Mary Turner, and had married my grandfather after the death of her resolution never to be reconciled to him. The child, christened Victor, was born eleven months after their reunion at the old farmhouse in Cheshire.

We are looking at the face of a young man, at sharp, clear eyes, an aquiline nose, a neat pencil moustache. He appears before us in the immaculate dress of his Cheshire regiment. We must ponder on the mystery of this youthful soldier's existence. His features closely resemble those of my father; they might, indeed, have been thought of as twin brothers from this similarity of appearance, but for the fact that they never shared a single tick of the earth's clock.

My father would sometimes speculate as to the character of his elder brother. It was a subject – alone amongst the many obsessions of his genealogical interests – which induced self-pitying reflections in him.

'But for Victor's death,' he would muse, 'I should never have been born – and, therefore both you and I, Tom, owe our existence to him. It is a curious thing to owe your life to someone you have never known, nor ever shall know. Yet I wish I had known him! I wish there had been a brother to look up to, because from the dawning of my consciousness, I spent my child-hood life in abject solitude.'

The nature of Victor's death had effectively banished the fact of it from the family history which my father was allowed to learn from his parents. His mother had mentioned it once when he was aged six – that he had had an elder brother who had died in a war. The convulsion of grief which had overwhelmed his mother upon her revelation of this had both terrified my father into asking nothing more about it, and had inadvertently made the subject for him one of intense private speculation. The sense of secrecy and mystery which seemed to enshroud this past event so impressed his young mind that it triggered his enduring fascination with both the history of his family and the history of the world. What had caused this war to be fought? What part had Victor played in it? He could only envisage his unknown brother dying a heroic death, such as he read about in boys' magazines. Yet all that remained was the name on a gravestone in the nearby churchyard, and – this led to some confusion in my father's mind as to where his brother's body actually lay – the same name, inscribed amongst seven others, upon a stone monument in the local village square.

Later, of course, in adolescence, Elias's monosyllabic responses to any questioning about the past drove my father to frustration and silent fury. It would be many years before he achieved a kind of revenge – if to establish the truth may be termed a revenge – upon this seeming conspiracy woven by those in authority, both in a military and a parental sense.

To catch a glimpse of the fleeting ghost which had been his brother's life, he would have to delve deep into the regimental archives; it was of prime importance to trace those men who had known Victor, and had survived the war. Sitting on benches in the grounds of nursing homes, or over pints of beer in social clubs, listening to the memories of old soldiers, my father learnt a truth in which there was no consolation. For Victor had not perished in the noble manner of the boyhood magazines.

*   *   *

In the twenty-fourth year of his life my Uncle Victor found himself standing on a platform of Crewe railway station, at four o'clock on a November morning in 1916. It had been snowing hard for three hours. Bright crystals fell from the soft blackness of the sky, to swirl momentarily in the golden, flickering gaslight before they dropped to earth, or settled on the caps and great-coats of a line of young men who formed a division of their Cheshire regiment. These men, huddled together in the snowstorm, had been standing by their kit bags for almost two hours, waiting to entrain, to journey via London to Dover, and then onwards to their ultimate destination: the Ypres salient.

They stamped their feet and hugged themselves against the bitter cold – shivering, teeth chattering, restless, bored and apprehensive, cursing the delay. Yet my Uncle Victor remained motionless, staring along the line of dark, silhouetted phantoms, before the faces of which the red-burning lights of cigarettes bobbed to and fro in the white-speckled darkness. These strokes of fire, like sudden wounds on the face of the night, began to mesmerize him. And in the air were ghostly voices, rising and falling in low murmur-ings, soft whispering, which – although he could not understand them – entranced and lulled him. Through clouded eyes he gazed across the railway tracks to the visible perimeter of a colourless world, all its subtle forms now buried under the deceptive snow.

And then he swayed, toppling against the soldier next to him, who instantly swore at him, then instinc-tively caught hold of his coat to prevent him from falling to the ground.

'Are you OK, mate?' he asked.

My Uncle Victor attempted to speak, but no sound

emerged from his throat, and the white and black and golden world swarmed before his eyes.

'He's fainted,' someone said. 'Sit him down.'

Wan disembodied faces glided in and out of his vision in the lamplight. He saw confused expressions, heard incomprehensible utterances. Only he knew that something impossible had befallen him. For in this snowbound world, which seemed set to freeze these men to their cores, his mind and his body had caught fire, as if by spontaneous combustion.

Then suddenly all attention was distracted from him by the thunderous noise of the train's arrival, which averted all faces and drowned all words as it drew up alongside the platform, testily gushing steam. Flecks of black smoke and showers of brilliant, evanescent sparks cascaded within the vortex of snowflakes.

The men began to board the train, and hands seized him, propelling him onwards, to set him eventually in a seat in the carriage. He lay, slumped there, his eyes closed and his breathing stertorous.

Still the train did not begin its long journey. Rumours began to be passed up and down the carriages – that there had been a derailment ahead, that there was a great congestion of troop trains attempting to converge on the Channel ports, that the battalion's posting to the Front was going to be delayed until some unspecified future date.

The men, now seated in the comparative comfort and warmth of this carriage, felt their mood brighten. Cigarettes were rolled and passed around; one man magically produced a hip flask, from which surreptitious sips were taken; playing cards flashed red and black in pale hands.

Those who had not felt compelled at once to close

their eyes and slumber grew ever more animated. Coarse anecdotes flew back and forth; crude jokes provoked helpless laughter, reckless boasts told of the revenge they would inflict on the enemy, whilst outside, the snow – all but forgotten by the men – still fell quietly and relentlessly.

Not long after five o'clock a tremendous jolt signalled their departure. As the train rumbled out of the station a shadow seemed to fall over the lightheartedness of the company, the conversations dwindled away, and those who had been sleeping opened their eyes, dragged from dreams by this sudden movement, to blink in the blue light of the carriage, and inwardly curse their exhaustion and their circumstances. For it appeared that this was no false start, after all, and their waking thoughts were focused again on the dangers which awaited them at the Front.

As they rolled slowly onwards, one man rubbed clear an oval space in the grey condensation of the carriage window. Gazing out, as though from a small porthole, and seeing only solid blackness, he declared that the snowstorm had abated, to which no-one proffered a response, since it now seemed a matter of petty significance.

The lulling motion of their cautious progress prompted the soldiers to finish their games of cards, stub out their cigarettes, settle back in their seats, and close their eyes.

Only one man in the carriage had remained utterly oblivious to everything which had been happening around him. My Uncle Victor had heard and seen nothing whatsoever, from the moment he had been manhandled on to the train. And once flung insensate into his seat, he had ceased to be the object of anybody's concern.

The train came to a shuddering halt. This sudden curtailing of the steady rhythm of its wheels roused a number of the men. They groaned, shifting in their seats, rearranging arms and legs which had grown stiff in the awkward positions in which they lay.

With the train at a standstill, a perfect silence suddenly invaded the carriage. But a few seconds later it was rent by a loud rattling exhalation. So chilling and unexpected was this sound that several men, not yet returned to profound sleep, at once opened their eyes. The sound came again, louder this time.

All around arose sudden groans of protest, angry calls for silence. But this horrifying noise persisted, delivered more urgently at rapid intervals. The soldier in the seat opposite to my Uncle Victor reached out an arm, intending to shake him violently. Instantly he recoiled at the sight of the great gouts of phlegm, flecked with blood, which had spilled down his chin and stained the lapel of his coat.

His terrified cry aroused others, who gathered around the pitiable figure of my uncle for the second time that night. His was a familiar face, yet none there could say they knew the man well, for he had never invited their close companionship. He had always been rather withdrawn in their presence, more inclined to read books than to indulge in camaraderie; he had shown no signs of physical prowess, but was easy-going, polite, humble.

The door of the carriage flew open with a crash, and a short stocky man, with cheeks newly shaven to ruddiness, and a small black moustache above a gaping red mouth seemed to explode amongst them, strafing them with swearwords. As this verbal shrapnel ricocheted down the compartment, the men learned that they had been rerouted, delayed and now were hopelessly behind their schedule.

The small crowd of men who were gathered around my uncle sprang stiffly erect, their anxious faces half turned towards their sergeant major. He advanced rapidly down the aisle, bursting them asunder, like a bowling ball through a group of skittles.

He leaned forward, staring implacably at the spectre of my Uncle Victor. He narrowed his eyes.

'He'll be no sodding use at the Front.'

Then he turned on his heels and marched away towards the front of the train, which – as if at some imperious yet unspoken command from him – juddered once more into motion.

Distracted by my uncle's plight yet helpless to know how to relieve it, the young men took their seats, lighting cigarettes and casting wary glances in his direction.

And now they notice that a dull light has returned to the world, by which they can see luminescent wastelands running unbroken to left and right, and here and there isolated farmhouses, the snow steeply banked against their walls, or a solitary tree, thrust as a giant skeletal hand out of the earth.

There is no medical officer on the train, and so the sergeant major returns to supervise the manoeuvre. He has instructed the locomotive driver to stop at the next station along the branch line. The train slows; the signboard announcing this destination appears outside the window, but the name is half-concealed where the snow has adhered to it, so the men know only that they have arrived at '----ston'.

At the sergeant major's instruction, the carriage door is opened and the same men who bore my Uncle Victor on to the train at Crewe now carry him off again. Their boots crunch into nine inches of snow. They slide and slither, unbalanced by the burden of his body, as they struggle to follow in their sergeant major's deep footprints towards a small draughty waiting room. The door is flung open and they haul my uncle within, laying him upon a slatted wooden bench. There is little they can do for the moment, but to wrap his coat more tightly about him. Someone murmurs about the necessity of fetching some help. Yet the sergeant major, without a word, at once returns to the train and embarks.

The men look at each other in astonishment. They fall into a brief discussion, then one runs along the platform to a stationmaster's small office and hammers upon its locked door. Another runs to a signal box, some fifty yards along the line, as the locomotive shatters the silence of the landscape with an eerie, impatient whistle. But this signal box, too, is silent and deserted, for both the stationmaster and the signalman know that on a morning such as this no milk train nor any local service can possibly run, and so each is soundly asleep in his bed.

The men regroup, to survey the deserted platform and the white countryside beyond. Some half a mile away lies a small hamlet, its houses all in darkness. Although they cannot know it, there is no doctor within the compass of a dozen miles.

Now the sergeant major is leaning out of the window of the train. He has watched all this activity keenly and knows no help is to hand, and so he begins to bellow at the men, ordering them to rejoin the train. There are murmurs of protest, oaths muttered under their breaths. The man who lies dying in the waiting room has never been the greatest of their friends. Yet he is a man, after all.

Slowly they clamber on to the train to take their seats. A whistle blows and they pull away. The soldiers gaze out of the windows in silence and disbelief.

A fortnight later a postman, labouring on his bicycle up a steep lane, steering unsteadily on the thawing snow, draws up before the house of Elias Crane. He opens the gate and passes between two strangely contorted trees, to knock at the door. He hands the official telegram to my grandfather. It informs him that, en route to France, his son contracted double pneumonia, and that 'whilst every medical facility and humane consideration at our disposal was afforded to him, he sadly was too advanced in his condition to be saved'.

Chapter Thirty-Three

Early one Saturday morning, late in October, I began the journey northwards. London receded in the rear-view mirror; and I joined the frantic dash along the motorway until I reached my exit from the madness, to pass through the last small town on the way to a destination which existed for me only in my dead father's memory.

Then I was steering along deserted minor roads, trammelled between thick hedgerows, under a vaporous sky. I stopped the car and turned off the engine in order to consult the map. Perfect stillness enveloped me; through the open windows wafted the intoxicating scents from the lane's verge, where wild flowers were beginning to decay. I remained there for several minutes, breathing in the essence of autumn, spellbound by the phrases of birds hidden in the thicket.

I knew that I was close to my destination as I traced the line of a railway track on the map. When I reached the top of the steep lane I could see its embankment curving hazily before me. From this vantage point I caught my first glimpse of a cluster of a dozen mid-century bungalows. I drove slowly past them. Squat, prefabricated, ugly by design, they seemed to be apologizing for their existence through the newness of their paintwork and their immaculately tended front gardens. Here then, the old farmhouse –

the place of my father's birth – had once stood, though not a vestige of it remained.

But I was more concerned to find a different, surviving remnant of that landscape and that world, and I quickly saw it, protruding solid and grey against the skyline above the tops of two plane trees.

This small stone-built church, with its square tower, stood, solidly buttressed – somehow sphinx-like in its aspect – amidst the quarter of an acre of its thinly populated graveyard. The gate of the churchyard was wedged open, and I walked along an overgrown footpath towards the western tower, noticing that the stone had weathered badly, that there was an air of desertion and dereliction about the building. I went around to the south side of the tower, to approach the porch.

A tattered notice in this porchway informed me that I stood on the threshold of a redundant church which had long ceased to be a living place of worship, but had been preserved because of its architectural merit. The notice informed me that I was free to enter here, but that I must respect the building and the grounds in which it stood, as a consecrated kingdom. So I turned the heavy handle on the reconstruction of its original medieval door, and stepped inside.

I found myself completely alone in the shadowy, cold, dank interior of that small, but almost complete, fourteenth-century church. There had been some minor restoration work in the nineteenth century, but my eye was caught by the ancient features of the place: the walls, coarsely and unevenly plastered; a font, five or six hundred years old, carved in low relief; and to either side of it two sets of three benches, of much the same age, roughly adorned with fleurs-de-lys poppy-heads.

The western end of the church was windowless, but as I walked towards its eastern precincts I saw how the drab light of this day was refracted marvellously through stained-glass depictions of Christ and His disciples, and of the Ascension. My footsteps fell on sixteenth-century brasses, set within the floor of the nave, and worn so smooth as to be indecipherable. Before me lay a plain pulpit, the zigzag of organ pipes, an ancient Communion table. I walked between the pews to read the texts of wall monuments which sped dignitaries, long since turned to dust, on their way to heaven.

As I turned to leave the church I felt, against my natural will – for this dead place seemed to strangle my spirit – the compulsion to sign the visitors' book and to deposit some change, in support of the Redundant Churches Fund, in the hungry mouth of a collection box set in the wall.

I stepped outside, breathing in the misty air and staring across the fields, where the forms of indistinct trees seemed bowed under their burden of dew. And so I strolled amongst the headstones until I came upon my grandmother's name, chiselled into a slab of black marble, standing slightly awry. 'MARY CRANE – Beloved wife of Elias – 1871-1925'. Below it I read: 'ELIAS CRANE – 1869-1946'. Adjacent to this was another headstone, which informed me that my Uncle Victor had lived between 1893 and 1916.

A wooden bench stood beneath one of the plane trees in the graveyard. As I sat there, shivering with the cold, enveloped in my solitude, I felt a great wave of sadness pass over me: I became the distracted ghost you sometimes see in country churchyards.

But once that was gone, in the stillness and the

silence, a sudden sense of relief – of finality – overtook me. I knew that, after all, the dust of Elias Crane lay mingled in the earth with that of my grandmother, Victoria Southley.

Chapter Thirty-Four

Victoria is sitting on the chaise longue, her face turned towards Elias, who stands, arms folded across his chest, in the doorway to his studio. They strain to make out each other's expression, for the room is only illuminated by the light of the fire now the winter's darkness has fallen swiftly.

'It's too late,' he says decisively.

'Too late!' she exclaims. 'If this thing is possible, it can *never* be too late!'

He draws a deep breath, then approaches her. He sits down beside her on the chaise longue, studying her profile, as she looks unseeingly into the red blistering faces in the coals. Her eyelids are fluttering rapidly as tears course down her cheeks, to splash on the hands she clenches in her lap. He senses the dreadful anguish which contracts her whole body with some unbearable implosion of grief. He places a hand on hers, which are silvered and chill from the falling tears. Over a month has passed, during which he can scarcely remember a waking moment when those eyes have not been inflamed, or brimful with her misery. He can scarcely believe the ability of any human being to cry so much, for so long, for his own stricken heart has seized up within him. All the well-tried consolations have failed here; and all his new inventions for soothing commiseration have not relieved the wound of her bereavement. Then, with his exasperation suddenly evaporating, words come tumbling from him. And although he cannot help adopting the parental tone of a father reasoning with a weeping child, he is telling her the truth – perhaps giving her more of himself than he has done for a quarter of a century.

'Do you remember,' he begins softly, 'that long ago you told me you were to be a mother? You – the daughter of a curate-in-charge! And I, the father – a painter, young and full of ambition then! So that it seemed to me we were both forfeiting our lives. I could not bear that revelation, because I was an unforgivable coward. And so I tried to rescue myself, in the full knowledge that I would ruin you by doing so. But I found at last that I would never grasp my salvation, wherever I went on this earth, until I returned to you. To make amends. I did so, only to discover that this child was a phantom of your imagination.'

The fire is burning down; suddenly the dark red coals subside in the grate, sending up gasps of blue fumes. One ember spills outwards, to sigh upon the hearthrug. Elias darts forward and flings it, in one swift motion, back into its grave, then resumes his place, sucking at his scorched fingertips.

'I was a different person then,' Victoria whispers.

'Be that as it may. You rejected me. All seemed utterly lost to me. Until the day you walked up the lane to this house. And in time there came the real child, who grew into an intelligent, sensitive young man, who has been killed in a senseless war.'

'The war will end one day,' comes her monotone.

Elias stands up suddenly, staring down piercingly at the back of Victoria's bowed head.

'And you think there will be no other wars to claim a

son to die in?' Now he cannot prevent his rage from dam-bursting. 'No! I tell you no! These children – real or imagined – seem to destroy my life. I cannot make any sense of the world. And so I refuse to go through it all again!'

His vehemence invites into this room a terrible, elongated silence. It must be filled somehow: if only by the spluttering of the coals, and the suppressed sob of his wife's unhappiness, smothering her emotion by pressing a lace handkerchief to her mouth.

Elias turns abruptly away from her. One might imagine that the matter has been settled, once and for all, as he begins to walk abruptly away; but in the doorway to his studio he turns on his heel.

'In any case,' he says, 'this is dangerous talk. It may kill *you*. After all, you are no longer a young woman.'

Instantly she jerks her head towards him, to berate him in a low yet decimating tone.

'You portray me so vividly. Yet you cannot imagine how empty my life is, now that Victor is dead. It is all simplicity to you. We have a house to live in, but has it ever occurred to you that we no longer have a life to share together within it? You complain that once you were so young and ambitious – to be a painter. But now you never paint. *What you paint, you destroy!* And always "the light is wrong"; "the subject will not work"; "the studio is too large"; "the studio is too small"; "nothing inspires me . . ."' Her voice broke into tremorous sobs. 'You are always so silent . . . so withdrawn. Well now—' she clasped her hands over her eyes – 'I'm just like you . . . my son was my work of art. But, unlike you, I would rather die than live without a child!'

She is staring at him defiantly, with such resolution

235

that he finds himself inescapably overcome by a freezing sense of fear.

'Yes. If you deny me this, I promise you I shall kill myself.'

Chapter Thirty-Five

So: 'I SHALL KILL MYSELF' brings back a resounding echo to Elias's mind. The grey wind-driven clouds, the relentless explosions of Atlantic waves breaking on a Provincetown beach. The sand in his shoes, on the palms of his hands, the cold mouth of a gun as it kisses his sweating temple.

Therefore my father never knew his elder brother, Victor, although – quite literally – he owed his life to him.

'Listen to me! Just listen to me!' I cry helplessly to my mother, who is seated opposite me at the kitchen table in that semi-detached house in Richmond, where all things know their places.

I have been talking at length, allowing speculation and hypothesis to run riot, in my attempt to blend some exotic stew from fact and imagination which may or may not approximate to the truth, until – suddenly appalled at myself – I pull up short. I rise like a starting ghost from the chair in which he habitually sat, as he penetrated the marble flesh of his upper thigh with a buckling hypodermic syringe, filled with a transparent solution of insulin.

'All my life I resisted it – and so did you. Yet here I am, boring you stiff with all these genealogical complications, with exactly the same pathological obsessiveness that he used to exhibit.'

My mother bursts out laughing: for the bright pain of our bereavement has become slowly and surely eclipsed through time.

'Picture it!' I exclaim, clutching my head in my hands. 'How on earth did I come to be mooching about in sub-zero temperatures, in the graveyard of some redundant church in the middle of nowhere, guessing the fates of all these characters whom I never knew – people who snuffed it aeons ago. Christ, there really must be something in the genes. I've become some frightening replication of him!'

My mother sniggers conspiratorially, and offers more tea from the pot. But time is running out for me, and so I drain the last mouthful from my cup. She comes to embrace me in farewell. Our cheeks meet, our arms enfold; there is the familiar scent of her powder, her perfume. My skin brushes hers, a reminder of our oneness, our singularity, our mortality.

And she waves me away, but with his favourite quotation vibrating in my mind: 'To be ignorant of what occurred before you were born is to remain always a child. For what is the worth of human life, unless it is woven into the life of our ancestors by the records of history?'

Chapter Thirty-Six

She was always there with him – the primary chord resounding through his childhood traumas and pleasures. It was she who sat on the side of his bed, without sleeping for nights on end, when he had become delirious with whooping cough. And she who filled with hot water the empty stone cider-jars to warm his bed. She who prayed incessantly, in darkness and light, after the doctor had struck a phosphorescent match in the blackness of the attic bedroom and held the hovering yellow light a mere three inches from his face, seeing no flicker of fear or any reaction in his clouded, staring eyes, and so had pronounced him beyond salvation.

It was she who intoned, over and over again, beside his inert body, the prayer: 'Please God, don't let him die.' It was she who watched him grow stronger, return to the world, attain consciousness again. Eventually he could scamper in her wake to the haunted, odorous realms of the outbuildings, where they would gather white and speckled eggs in the hayloft, or milk the cows in the shadowy, pungent shippen where the beasts stood steaming in their stalls at dawn, their milk streaming in dazzling white spurts into the galvanized pail.

It was she whose skin he seemed perpetually to be pressed against, whose aura happily imprisoned him, as he grew up in that ancient, creaking house which was always redolent of baking bread, of the butter and cheeses she made. Unaware that he was loved by her, first and foremost, simply because he had been invented against very difficult odds, rather than for the character into which he slowly grew – an obedient child, sweet-tempered, intelligent, insatiably curious about all things – he was able to bask in this maternal devotion.

It was she whose hand clasped his as they walked along the lanes in all seasons and all weathers, as he seemed to be setting out upon a voyage of discovery, to learn the naming of the universe. She who taught him to read, to write, to count. And she who endeavoured to protect him from the strange phenomenon of his father – a shadowy, fearsome figure who stalked the perimeter of his infantile experiences, a distant, unwelcome intruder in their home . . .

And so I must bring my father back to life, dreaming him downwards through layers of time, so that he is now a boy of seven years old, standing – or more accurately lying – unwittingly on the threshold of a great tragedy in his innocent life . . .

It is close to midnight, and my father is fast asleep in bed. Were he awake, he might hear the deadened footfalls of Elias Crane as he strides across the cobbled farmyard, his boots crunching on freshly-fallen snow, his cheroot sparking in the thick blackness, ice crystals whirling like a swarm of white-winged moths about the oil lamp he holds aloft in his left hand. Onward he goes, a dark figure in a gyrating circle of yellow light . . .

Regardless of the weather, he feels compelled to take these nightly perambulations. There is a moon-bright frost, holding rigid the brittle carpet of grass beneath his feet, as he sets off to pace around the shrunken boundaries of his kingdom. These walks are always brooding escapes, during which he bitterly evaluates the course of his life and the hopelessness of his circumstances.

For all too soon he will be rebuffed by the thirty-foot-high brick walls of engine sheds and warehouses, which sprang out of the earth on the land that his mother sold to the railway company over thirty years ago – before she went to Chester, with the intention of dying.

Elias was never to see her alive again, following her departure for her sister's sanctuary. He had written to her once, in the early spring of 1891:

My dear Mother,
    I am well, and I hope you, too, are in good health. Incidentally, I have married a woman named Mary Turner.
    Yours,
    Elias.

Several weeks later, she replied:

My dear Son,
    I am glad to hear that you are in good health. Unfortunately – or happily, depending on my mood – I am decidedly not so.
    Your Mother.

A week after this exchange she died, and her sister

took the liberty of burying her first, before she deigned to inform Elias of his mother's death.

He stands still, breathing the frigid late autumn air, blinking against the frozen rain of snowflakes which settles upon his eyelashes.

And he is brooding still on the problem of time – how so much of it has flowed by him, bringing him a first son, who was cruelly taken from him; and then a second son, who now sleeps in the attic room of the farmhouse, but for whom, in his emotional paralysis, he can feel very little.

For this son's conception had nothing to do with love. It was simply a product of a compromise on Elias's behalf, after his will had been relentlessly besieged for months by Victoria's demands for a child. In the whole of this second fatherhood, he will experience only two genuine moments of feeling. A chill will pass over his heart on the day his son is called up for the war; and on the day my father returns home, miraculously alive, a great sense of relief will possess Elias – that history has not repeated itself. Both these aberrations in feeling will be consummately disguised.

But what of the rest of that time? How has he come to squander it, in so much dedication to useless ends? For all is locked inside him. He has read voraciously; now he is an erudite man. Yet he resembles nothing more than a monastic scholar, trapped in a vow of silence towards the human race. He has learned classical languages; his knowledge of art history is profound; and yet his own inspiration to paint has entirely evaporated.

And what has time done to love? Now, standing in

this empty, frost-bound field, the earth beneath his feet iron-hard, he can only look back to the days when he was a young, ambitious man, strolling through the blinding white sun-filled streets of Penzance and Newlyn, Grez, Barbizon, or Pont-Aven, alive to the possibilities of life and love. For if he had ever truly loved, he had loved Victoria Southley, who had commanded all those contrary currents of emotion which had first swept him towards her, then had cast him far distant, only to speed him back inexorably into her thrall.

Now such intense passions seem alien to his heart. Love had once transformed him into the man who – seared in his soul – had returned, to linger hesitantly for hours upon end at the windswept corner of Chywoone Hill and Old Paul Street; had compelled him to write four last, desperate lines to her, from a squalid room in the Ocean Rest House. Yet those four lines – which had represented no inspired composition of a despairing man, no beautiful, mellifluous plea for mercy – had ultimately worked their simple magic. For he had merely written four proper nouns: the name of the farmhouse, of the lane along which it stood, of the nearest village, and of the county in which all of them were situated.

So, when he was returning, some months later, from a hot spring morning spent desultorily painting in the fields, he had encountered the figure of Victoria Southley, who was standing – a look of consternation upon her face – by the garden gate, staring questioningly at the house. In frozen amazement, easel, palette, paints had cascaded from his grip, to spill upon the hard, riveted lane, as he went forward to embrace her. Pure joy and triumph had possessed him then. To the end of his life, he would recognize that moment as the pinnacle of his earthly happiness.

So three decades have flown to bring him here, to this field across which he now walks in the falling snow. Time's erosion of passion and happiness seems to him complete: for he had loved Victoria Southley; yet he had married Mary Turner.

And now that Elias is a man in his mid-fifties, he has come to accept that, spiritually, he has inherited the seafarer's destiny – to be a man banished from his natural way of life, severed from all earthly joys, fated to be alone for ever. Always in the back of his mind, he hears the beating of white waves on alien shores; the howling of snowstorms; and the forlorn cries of sea birds.

He turns back from the boundary of his domain, and retraces his steps towards the glowing lights of the farmhouse.

Chapter Thirty-Seven

Then something happens. Elias hears a distant, high-pitched cry and stops, listening to the dark silence all around him. Perhaps an animal has been snared in a farmer's trap; or seized in the beak or jaws of some invisible predator. After a few moments, he sets forth again; then the cry is repeated, a louder, somehow more human sound, and one which seems to come from the direction of the farmhouse, to which he is now very close. Eerily, it is answered at once by the shrill whistle of a mail train, approaching fast out of the night.

Elias begins to run and the sudden jolting motion extinguishes the lamp. He blunders onwards across the cobbled yard, slipping and sliding on the snow, making for the lighted window. The train thunders by behind him, so that he does not glimpse a different rectangle of blazing light – hurtling as if disembodied through the blackness – in which is imprisoned the figure of a man, his naked arms and torso blood-red, as he energetically shovels coal from the tender to the fire-box.

That second cry in the darkness has awoken my father from his dreams. He hears running footsteps cross the cobbled yard and then the slamming of the door below. Alarmed, he rises from his bed, hearing next the muffled sounds of his father shouting. Then a crash, as though some heavy piece of furniture has been overturned. He stands shivering both from the cold air and the fearful possibility that his parents – neither of whom he has ever heard raise a voice in anger – are enacting some violent argument.

Perhaps he himself has done something wrong, and is the very cause of all this rage? He stays cowering in the darkness of his room, anticipating the sounds of his father swiftly mounting the stairs to turn his wrath upon him.

Yet no footsteps come. There is another crash, of a vase or ornament shattering on the floor. And then he decides that he must act, for his father may be hurting his mother, and so he must save her.

It is a game he has often played: to creep as silently as a cat about the house, to approach his mother furtively when her back is turned, and seize her around the waist so that she cries out with surprise, then chases him as he runs away. Once he is caught, they embrace in exhilarating laughter.

Now the game is to be played in earnest. My father stealthily unlatches the door, slips out in bare feet on to the landing, where he pauses, listening intently. Light flows upwards from the hall below, and he begins his descent in agile movements. The third, fourth, eighth and tenth stairs he knows are wont to creak, and he skips over them, finally coming to a halt in the hallway. Suddenly the tall grandfather clock, its face adorned with smiling suns and silver moons, chimes the half-hour. He starts at the peal of its bells, but is at once distracted by two things: the first waft of a strange, pungent odour on the chill air, and the sound of an insistent whimpering from beyond the closed door of the drawing-room.

He tiptoes to this door, which all at once bursts open, and a dreadful spectre – his father, wild-eyed, wreathed in black smoke – bursts from the room, colliding with his own son, knocking the boy to the floor. And now everything seems to happen at once, in one gigantic assault upon my father's senses. Sprawled upon the floor, the breath ripped out of him, he feels his father pull him roughly to his feet. And Elias is shrieking at him, that he must go from the house, and run far away, and not return until dawn. And his father's face is contorted and blistered. Meanwhile through the door a sea of smoke is pouring, laden with that odd, acrid odour, to swirl in the dull light of the oil lamp, and through its shifting veils black motes are raining. He sees that a writing table lies overturned on the drawing-room floor.

In the next instant his father is propelling him forcibly along the hall towards the front door, and then he is outside, racing down the garden path in terror, with his father's footsteps in close pursuit. He wrenches open the garden gate, swerves to the left and flies up the lane. Glancing back, he sees that his father has run away in the opposite direction, towards the nearest village.

So my father, ankle-deep in snow, wearing only a cotton nightshirt, blinded by tears, dashes to and fro in the darkness, wailing at the top of his voice. He cannot make any sense of those rapid, disjointed events – why there should have been a sea of smoke, why he should have been hurled from the house, why his father had screamed at him. What terrifying apparition had his father seen, to give him the face of a madman? And how could he himself be to blame for whatever had happened this night?

*   *   *

The house lay out of sight beyond a copse of trees. As my father's anxiety grew, he seemed, astonishingly, to be able to reason more clearly. Of course, it was simple. The house had caught fire. His father had sent his mother away to safety, then had tried to put out the blaze. Having failed to do so, he was just about to rush upstairs to save his son. That was why he had told my father to flee, and not to return for a long time. Then he had run off to fetch help from the village.

And yet the house was on fire! He ran back down the lane, until the building came into sight. But no towering flames leapt into the sky, and the drawing-room window stood out in the darkness as a single, un-wavering square of light. He went closer, to stand by the garden gate. The scene remained unchanged before his eyes, as he stood there for several minutes. Should he enter the house? He was almost on the point of doing so, when he remembered that his father had forbidden this.

So he waited, and time stopped, for no-one came or went, no snowflakes fell, no sound was heard, but for his own violent shivering. Then he began to be frightened for another reason: his imagination told him that his mother would surely have found him by now, unless he had died and become a ghost, for ghosts must live alone, and Hell is either very hot, or very cold.

He began to weep and to pace up and down the lane, but then the instinct for survival brought its inspiration. Inside the old barn, he groped in the blackness towards the ladder to the loft. Once he had ascended there he lay down, covering himself with a deep blanket of hay, and misery dragged him down into sleep.

* * *

The sound of horses' hoofs and carriage wheels upon the cobblestones of the farmyard cause my father to start from unconsciousness and rush to the small unshuttered window in the gable end of the barn. It is almost dawn, and in the gathering light he sees his father dismount from the carriage in the company of two men. Immediately he calls out to his father, who wheels around, looking upwards to the source of the voice, seeing his son's pale face framed in the window.

'Stay there,' he says sternly, 'until I come to you.'

The men disappear into the house. My father resolves to stay awake, but as the minutes and then the hours pass, he is defeated by exhaustion. He awakens again to the noise of the carriage departing. Suddenly the door of the barn opens, his father calls to him, and he scrambles to the edge of the hayloft and down the ladder. He turns to face his father, who crouches down, so that they stare straight into each other's eyes.

My father recoils, for in the dawn light he can clearly see that his father's hair is scorched, that his eyebrows have been burnt away, that his cheek is horribly blistered, that his expression is wild and haggard.

'Your mother is dead.'

Chapter Thirty-Eight

Long before the plane trees were planted in the
churchyard, half a century before the building was
vested in the Redundant Churches Fund, three figures
stood, black statues alone in an impossibly white
world, beside an open grave, as the priest intoned the
order for the burial of the dead.

'*And though after my skin worms destroy this
body . . .*'

Elias stared into the pit, lined as though with white
wool by the falling snow. His son regarded the priest
with an unwavering stare of hatred, assuming that this
tall thin man in black, with his nose running, his shaking hand which held the book close to his face, his
nose inflamed by tiny rivulets of red veins, was yet
another part of the conspiracy to take his mother from
him. We can only speculate as to the appalling fancies
which have gripped his young heart during the terrible
days which preceded this funeral. Lying awake at
night in his attic room, his thoughts must have been
hooked by cruel question marks. What if the earth
were frozen solid, so solid that no deep grave could be
dug? And if that were not the case, what if the grave
had been filled with the night's fall of snow, and could
not be located again? Would they have to leave his
mother's body above ground, until the snow melted?
And if they did, what fate might befall it at the hands of

grave-robbers, or the jaws of dogs and foxes?

'My heart was hot within me, and while I was thus musing the fire kindled . . .'

The service is drawing to its close, the priest's delivery accelerating in direct proportion to his discomfort, so that words run together, syllables slide and slither into one another, until his utterances seem nonsensical.

'I heard a voice from heaven, saying unto me, Write, From henceforth blessed are the dead . . .'

Father and son leave the churchyard, walking slowly along the lane to the farmhouse. No words are spoken; each seems to carry an immense burden of silence upon his bowed shoulders. They stop at the garden gate and momentarily look into each other's eyes. Elias almost voices the paradox which has tormented him on the short walk home: 'That she should have died in fire, yet be buried in ice'.

But he does not, instead opening the gate, and walking slowly towards the house.

Chapter Thirty-Nine

The Dolphin tavern by Penzance harbour can prove to be a pleasant place to take a quiet drink or two at lunchtime, especially when the tourist season has drawn to a close. But those who have recently departed have forfeited their share in a matchless September day, for the sun is raining molten gold upon the town, and in Mount's Bay the waves roll in, as long white spokes of some massive, blue, slowly-revolving wheel.

In the Dolphin today there are no rowdy darts-players, electronic-games addicts, or jukebox fiends in evidence to disturb its pleasant quietness. I sit alone at my table in the cool, darkened interior, hunched over the manuscript I have written. I reach the final chapter, and put the work aside.

My father enters, dressed in his shapeless tweed jacket and his battered trilby hat. He buys a pint of bitter at the bar, then approaches, to sit down beside me. He lights his pipe and, picking up the sheaf of papers, settles back in his seat and begins to read.

Although he will never see me, nor speak to me again, I turn to him to tell him that it has not been in vain: that he conjured up a host of unremembered people – the ghosts of those long since under the earth – to make them live again.

He ignores me, merely nodding or grunting as he

leafs through the manuscript, here and there jotting down comments in the margin in red ink. Eventually he lays the novel aside.

'Not bad, Tom,' he murmurs to himself. 'But it needs a lot more research, son.'

Then he drains his glass, rises and makes for the door.

I am alone once more: my father has gone for ever, fleeing with the hosts who can bequeath to us only the ruins of time.

Vermin Blond
by Richard Davis

'Everyone called him Gaby. To have known him meant to be uneasy ever after . . .'

Why should a middle-aged solicitor abandon his wife, his home and his job, to dispose of a dead friend's estate? To find the answer Mark Palfreyman must delve into his past and confront its demons.

He looks back to 1968 and his last year at St Clement's, a boys' public boarding school, and the people who dominated his adolescence: his family, well-meaning but an embarrassment; Ambrose, the crushingly rude senior tutor; Judy, the history master's girlfriend and Mark's 'Ideal Woman'. But looming over them all is Martin Gabriel – Gaby – the rebel angel who dazzles man and woman, master and pupil alike. Mark, too, is captivated, but as he is drawn into Gaby's select circle, he glimpses a darker, grimmer side to the 'vermin blond' charmer.

VERMIN BLOND brilliantly captures the claustrophobic atmosphere of an all-male society. Its savage denouement is at once believable and shocking.

'I was impressed by the assured authorial voice, and completely gripped by the characters throughout'
Robert Carver, *Observer*

'Davis knows his patch well and acutely observes the tribal alliances, cold-shower ethics and repressed sexuality of this warping environment'
Nicholas Marston, *GQ*

0 552 99484 7

BLACK SWAN

Firedrake's Eye
by Patricia Finney

'In the same league as Rose Tremain's *Restoration*, and
Umberto Eco's *The Name of the Rose*'
Kate Saunders, *Cosmopolitan*

In the autumn of 1583, in the fetid alleyways of
Whitefriars, the loyal courtier Simon Ames is viciously
beaten. The random prey of footpads – or victim of a
subtly treasonous act? A nonsense poem written by the
lunatic Tom O'Bedlam has become a favourite of
London's ballad-sellers. Who has taken the wild
meanderings of a madman so seriously – and why?

Following a trail of murder, treason and terror, Ames and
his dubious friend Becket set out to uncover the truth. But
as they dig deep into the human midden that is
Elizabethan London, puzzle becomes enigma, then riddle.
What is the secret at the heart of the pageantry to be
paraded before the Queen at the Accession Day Tilts? Who
is Tom and what does his ballad mean?

'The plot builds ingeniously to a Day-of-the-Jackal
denouement . . . To read this book is to live for a while in
another London, a place that is credible and entertaining.
For all its dirt and danger there is a rich pleasure in losing
yourself in its tortuous streets'
Nicolette Jones, *Sunday Times*

'Historical fiction the way it should be written . . . A talent
for writing espionage makes her the le Carré of the 16th
century'
Ruth Rendell, *Daily Telegraph*

'Compulsive . . . (Finney) has succeeded in conjuring up
the filthy crowded splendour of 16th century London'
P.J. Kleeb, *Times Literary Supplement*

Available from Black Swan in March 1993

0 552 99508 8

BLACK SWAN

A SELECTION OF FINE NOVELS AVAILABLE FROM BLACK SWAN

THE PRICES SHOWN BELOW WERE CORRECT AT THE TIME OF GOING TO PRESS. HOWEVER TRANSWORLD PUBLISHERS RESERVE THE RIGHT TO SHOW NEW RETAIL PRICES ON COVERS WHICH MAY DIFFER FROM THOSE PREVIOUSLY ADVERTISED IN THE TEXT OR ELSEWHERE.

☐ 99198 8	THE HOUSE OF THE SPIRITS	*Isabel Allende*	£5.99
☐ 99313 1	OF LOVE AND SHADOWS	*Isabel Allende*	£5.99
☐ 99459 6	SHINING AGNES	*Sara Banerji*	£4.99
☐ 99498 7	ABSOLUTE HUSH	*Sara Banerji*	£4.99
☐ 99484 7	VERMIN BLOND	*Richard Davis*	£5.99
☐ 99466 9	A SMOKING DOT IN THE DISTANCE	*Ivor Gould*	£6.99
☐ 99487 1	JIZZ	*John Hart*	£5.99
☐ 99169 4	GOD KNOWS	*Joseph Heller*	£3.95
☐ 99195 3	CATCH-22	*Joseph Heller*	£5.99
☐ 99409 X	SOMETHING HAPPENED	*Joseph Heller*	£5.99
☐ 99209 7	THE HOTEL NEW HAMPSHIRE	*John Irving*	£5.99
☐ 99369 7	A PRAYER FOR OWEN MEANY	*John Irving*	£6.99
☐ 99205 4	THE WORLD ACCORDING TO GARP	*John Irving*	£6.99
☐ 99130 9	NOAH'S ARK	*Barbara Trapido*	£4.99
☐ 99056 6	BROTHER OF THE MORE FAMOUS JACK	*Barbara Trapido*	£4.99

All Black Swan Books are available at your bookshop or newsagent, or can be ordered from the following address:

Corgi/Bantam Books,
Cash Sales Department
P.O. Box 11, Falmouth, Cornwall TR10 9EN

UK and B.F.P.O. customers please send a cheque or postal order (no currency) and allow £1.00 for postage and packing for the first book plus 50p for the second book and 30p for each additional book to a maximum charge of £3.00 (7 books plus).

Overseas customers, including Eire, please allow £2.00 for postage and packing for the first book plus £1.00 for the second book and 50p for each subsequent title ordered.

NAME (Block Letters) ....

ADDRESS ....

....